SLOW BURGESS

SLOW BURGESS

CHARLES ALDEN SELTZER

CUTTING EDGE

ISBN-13: 978-1-954840-61-4

Published by
Cutting Edge Books
PO Box 8212
Calabasas, CA 91372
www.cuttingedgebooks.com

TABLE OF CONTENTS

CHAPTER ONE

Big Dave Dawley stopped at the cigar counter of the City Hotel. Following his usual custom, he lit the cigar and, puffing hugely at it, cast a slow, amused glance around him at the other guests of the place. For Dawley, besides being huge physically, was Paro City's big man.

"He's a schemer all right," remarked the man behind the cigar counter, as Dawley went out. "Slick an' deep."

Another man cleared his throat.

"If I knowed as much as Dawley knows about what's goin' to happen to this town, I'd sure make a cleanup!"

"Meanin' the railroad, I reckon," grinned the cigar-counter man. "Well, I reckon we're outsiders in *that* deal."

"An' in a heap of other deals that Dawley's swingin'," said the other lugubriously. "He's got more irons in the fire than we've got any idea of."

Dawley had halted on the wooden platform that fringed the front of the hotel. His gaze swept Paro City with the calculating interest that was always in his eyes when he was thinking of the town's future.

Down the street a glaring sign met his gaze: "The Dawley Saloon and Dance Hall." Dawley's eyes glittered. The place was exceedingly profitable. Most of his other ventures were likewise profitable.

He smiled as his gaze roved over the broad sweep of plain that began at the edge of the town, stretching away into hazy nothingness toward the eastern horizon. From that direction would come the railroad. And the railroad would make Paro City. And when the making process was finished, Dawley would cash in on his investments.

Dawley's gaze merely swept Paro City's huddled frame shanties. His eyes, glowing with the flame of desire, rested upon the substantial brick building across the street from him, with its broad, gilt sign over the door: "The Burgess Bank."

For a week the bank had been closed to the citizens of Paro City, following the death of its owner, William Burgess. Two men—Galfant and Glenmere—that Dawley had brought from Yuma upon Judge Quinn's request for accountants who would make a comprehensive report of the institution's condition—were working inside the banking room. Dawley could see the men as they moved to and fro. Dawley stepped across the street and entered the bank.

Galfant, the taller of the two men, opened the door for him. He grinned mildly and intimately at Dawley.

"Find anything?" questioned Dawley.

"Nothing. We've combed the place clean. There ain't a scrap of paper anywhere that would show what old Burgess wanted to do with his property."

Dawley moistened his lips.

"All right," he said shortly, "keep working. I'll report to Judge Quinn."

He stepped out through the door and walked down the street, smiling faintly. A few minutes later he was confronting Judge Quinn in the little frame courthouse.

"Quinn," he said, "Bill Burgess died without making a will. Or, if he did make one, nobody has come forward with it.

They would have come forward if a will had been made. That's a cinch! Burgess had a son named Clay. But the son has not been heard from in seven years—or since I have been here. To my knowledge, that is. And to nobody else's, that I've heard of. He must be dead. Burgess had no other relatives. That I have been able to discover by going through his papers."

Judge Quinn gasped. He was startled and dismayed over Dawley's ruthless and unauthorized interference in Burgess' affairs.

"You—you did that!" he said. "Why, it's illegal! The court hasn't authorized—"

"Forget it!" grinned Dawley. "Somebody has got to take the Burgess estate in hand. Make me Burgess' executor until such a time as his heir appears and is duly identified and qualified."

Judge Quinn stiffened, and for an instant it appeared he would defy Dawley. But a long glance into the other's smiling, determined eyes decided the judge, and he made out the necessary papers.

Still smiling, Dawley returned to the bank. He went directly to the safe, opened it, and scrutinized every paper.

Dawley discovered that Burgess' holdings were larger and more valuable than he had thought. The discovery sent a pulse of joy and avarice over him.

That night, after going over the books and talking long with Glenmere, he sat in the directors' room of the bank for a long time, staring out through the front windows into the deepening dusk that was enveloping Paro City, his thoughts on the missing heir. He knew more of the whereabouts of the heir than he had told Judge Quinn. A glare, cold and sullen, came into his eyes, and a passion, which boded no good for the heir, gripped his heart.

The next morning he appeared before Judge Quinn, showing the latter a Burgess Bank letterhead upon which was written:

MY WILL

In the event of my son, Clay Burgess, failing to appear to claim my estate, it is my wish that all my property be turned over to my good friend, Dave Dawley.

(Signed) WILLIAM BURGESS

"I found this among the Burgess papers," he told Judge Quinn. "I suppose it will have to be recorded to make it hold. Record it."

Judge Quinn demurred, looking up at Dawley suspiciously. "It isn't regular, Dawley; it hasn't been sworn to by a notary. It might be a forgery."

"Do you think I would forge it?" demanded Dawley. His big hands went out and were laid on Judge Quinn's shoulders, and his eyes, smoldering with malevolence, bored into those of the other.

"No-o," faltered the judge. "Not you—of course. I didn't mean that. I—I meant that some unscrupulous friend might have—"

"You're a hell of a Christian to speak of scruples," sneered Dawley. "I remember a time when you were managing an estate in Phoenix, jointly with the governor, when your scruples weren't so active as now. Bah! You'd like to be an honest crook, eh? Record that, and let me hear no more about it!"

"It wouldn't hold in law," declared the judge, his face ghastly with a fear that someone might have overheard Dawley—for the latter's voice had boomed and rumbled through the room. "It simply must bear the signature of a witness and the seal of a notary."

"Wait a minute, then!" Dawley went out and shortly afterward returned with Ben Davis, the justice of the peace.

He sat down at Judge Quinn's desk at Dawley's invitation, but got up quickly after reading the paper Dawley laid before him.

"That's an infernal forgery!" he charged. "Bill Burgess never signed no paper like that!" There was a righteous rage in the glitter of his grey eyes. "You can't git me to put the seal on no such lyin' thing as that!"

"Don't lose your temper, old man," cautioned Dawley sulkily. "You oldtimers are apt to think everything crooked that you know nothing about. You will notice that this paper is witnessed by Dal Coleman—and you know Coleman, don't you?"

"I know Coleman to be the sneakiest crook in Paro City—outside of yourself!" sniffed Davis. He stiffened to belligerent rigidity at Dawley's short, aggressive movement toward him, and went on: "Bill Burgess didn't have as much use for Dal Coleman as he had for a rattlesnake. No more'n he had use for you! Which means that he wouldn't will you none of his money if the choice laid between you an' a prairie dog. An' when the time comes to talk about wills I'll have somethin' to say myself. Don't forget that!" He marched out of the room, muttering.

Dawley looked after him with a smooth, malicious smile. Then he turned to the judge, saying quietly:

"Record it. My word is as good as Ben Davis'!" He walked to the door. "No monkey business, Quinn. Remember!"

There was no fear of legal punishment in Dawley's soul, nor was there any physical apprehension to deter him. For Dawley feared no man.

He had not forgotten Ben Davis. Nor had he forgiven him. One morning about a week after the scene in the courthouse he walked into the tumble-down shanty which answered as office and living room for Davis. He did not sit down, but walked to where Davis was sitting, and leaned both hands on the desk, smiling blandly into Davis' face.

"Did you get it, Ben?"

Davis reddened. "What you talking about?"

"About you. I'm asking about the governor's order revoking your justice license. Did you get it?"

"Yes—damn you!" said Davis. "I was thinkin' of quittin' anyway."

Dawley straightened, laughing.

"So much the better. I was talking with Mogridge this morning. You know Mogridge, of course. He's the new sheriff. He's been looking over some old records, from down Las Vegas way. Pretends he discovered some evidence incriminating you in some shady deal or other. All in his mind, I reckon, but he's an obstinate cuss when he's engaged in what he calls his duty. But in my talk with him I suggested that perhaps if you'd get out of the country he'd not molest you. Going?"

"Yes!" snapped Davis. "I was gittin' ready—been considerin' it for a long time. Too many crooks here—like you. But the new sheriff ain't drivin' me out—understand that! I ain't done nothin'—an' I understand. It's a frame-up. I'm goin', but if there's a word said that you've run me out I'm comin' back—heeled!"

He dropped a hand to his hip, and it came up, holding a six-shooter.

"I've had a heap of experience, packin' this. It's trained to fan the guts of stiffs like you, an' it's yearnin' for action. I reckon we understand each other."

"No doubt of it, Ben," laughed Dawley. "Well, so long, Ben. No hard feelings."

Dawley stepped out of the door, swinging nonchalantly down the street. Davis looked after him with grudging admiration.

"He carries it off good!" he said; "damned good! He's slick an' cool. But if that young Clay Burgess ever comes back, an' he's got the kind of nerve the old man had, there'll be two cool an' nervy ones lockin' horns. It'll be some battle, man!" He chuckled, his imagination drawing pictures for him. "Some battle—or I'm a gopher!"

CHAPTER TWO

Late in the afternoon on the day of Dawley's visit to his office, Ben Davis rode up to the door of a cabin that stood at the edge of a section of broken country northeastward from Paro City.

There was a grim smile on Davis' face, which mingled strangely with an embarrassed flush as, sitting in the saddle, he hallooed and waited for an answer.

The answer came in the shape of a comely, brownhaired young woman who suddenly appeared in the doorway. Her eyes widened and danced with delight when she saw him.

"Why, it's Ben Davis!" she cried. "Get down and come right in. You are just in time for supper!"

He said nothing about what had happened to him until after the conclusion of the meal. Then, responding to the look of inquiry that the young woman threw at him, Davis grinned in a crestfallen manner.

"There's another candidate for Williams' cache, Della," he said.

"Who?" questioned the girl.

"Me." A flush of color suffused Davis' face.

"You've had trouble with Dawley? What about?"

Davis told her.

"Looks like Dawley's goin' to grab the Burgess property," he concluded.

"He can't!" declared the girl spiritedly.

"They ain't nothin' to prevent him," declared Davis. "Bill Burgess always had a lot of faith in his boy, Clay. Always said he'd come back. They wasn't no hard feelin's when the boy went away. He just wanted to mosey around independent. Don't know as I blame him.

"Bill said he'd be back. An' mebbe he will. But there ain't nothin' that can be done unless he does come back. Bill Burgess didn't trust that little whippersnapper of a judge, Quinn. Bill made his will, leavin' everything to Clay. But he wouldn't let the will go to court, bein' afraid Quinn an' Dawley would tamper with it. I've got it.

"But I can't turn it over to *that* court. I've told you what Dawley's done. They mean to kill young Clay—if he comes back. That's what the will that Dawley's made means. They ain't nothin' to do but wait. Mebbe young Clay *will* come back—his dad sent a letter to him at Yuma—where Clay was to stop an' ask if he ever come that way—tellin' Clay he wasn't feelin' any too well an' askin' him to come home. Three months ago, that was. Mebbe Clay will come. If he don't, I reckon Dawley's got things his own way. They ain't nothin' we can do."

The girl sat tense, her hands gripping the edge of the table, her face flushed, passionate resentment in her eyes.

"You shall not go to Williams' cache, Ben!" she declared. "Dawley has sent too many good men there, to become outlaws! He shan't send you. Before daddy died he told me to ask you to come over here, to stay with me—to help me. I want you to do as he said. And we'll fight Dawley, Ben—if we have to! All alone, if we must!

"You'll stay—won't you, Ben? You won't let Dawley run you out of the country?"

Davis grinned mirthlessly. "My runnin' days are over, Della," he said. "Dawley ain't got me scared none. Why," he added, his voice softening, "I reckon I was friend enough to Elam Bowen not to desert his daughter when she needs someone to stand by her!"

Riding due east, two days out of Yuma, where he had read his father's letter, Clay Burgess' wide-brimmed sombrero was tilted to keep the sun off the back of his neck. His face was lean, strong, and russet-brown from exposure. Odd little wrinkles were around Burgess' eyes. But though the wrinkles made him look at least ten years older than his twenty-seven, they were not agewrinkles; they were the creases that come from much squinting against the sun in open places, and from their owner's habit of indulging in much quizzical thought. Yet they were misleading until one caught the virile sparkle of his eyes.

Burgess was tall, big-boned, and muscular. His shoulders bulged the woollen shirt which, open at the throat, contrasted darkly with the scarlet neckerchief he wore. His waist was slim, and the cartridge belt at his middle sagged with the weight of the two heavy pistols of his hips. His legs, long, were well-muscled and sturdy.

The trail merged with another as he rode eastward, and from a slight rise he could see other trails winding toward a point of convergence far into the distance. He knew where the point was—beyond a plain of uncropped salt grass, where some timber fringed a dry arroyo. He had ridden there many times.

As he rode on the place became well-remembered, familiar. He grinned as he rode, a pulse of eagerness shooting through him, for now that he was near home the spell of it began to seize upon him and make him happy.

But he went onward slowly, for the note of anxiety in his father's letter did not disturb him. Burgess thought, reading between the lines, that he detected a wistful yearning on his father's part rather than a concern for the health that he thought was deserting him.

Burgess smiled often, remembering the day of his departure from Paro City ten years before. There had been no harsh words—his father had realized that the wanderlust had seized his son, and had sent him upon his way with a smile.

Burgess had dwelt upon that smile many times, but deepest in his recollection had been the slight wistfulness of it. But Burgess would repay his father—that he vowed earnestly as he rode.

The long western twilight fell before he came in sight of town, and when he was still ten miles away the dense blackness of the night enwrapped him. But town was near now—nearer than it had been in many years—and in Burgess' heart grew a hunger nameless and gripping.

CHAPTER THREE

Dawley breakfasted at the City Hotel across the street from the bank—he had removed all his belongings to the rooms above the bank. Then he walked over to the bank where, behind the wire wicket, he talked with the cashier, Glenmere.

"Growing, eh?" he said, looking over the deposit slips.

"Some," grinned the other.

Dawley looked with level eyes at Glenmere.

"Jay Hammond will be in today. His note is due. Demand. Send him to me."

The cashier nodded.

At a little after ten o'clock Dawley was sitting in the directors' room looking across the table at a tall, bearded man who had been ushered into his presence by the cashier.

The man was plainly anxious, for during the time that Dawley was looking over some papers on his desk, seemingly in ignorance of the man's presence, the latter eyed him furtively and hopefully.

"Well, Hammond?" said Dawley finally.

"My note is due today," blurted Hammond. "I—I suppose you know that. I want to renew it; I've got the interest."

"Your note was for twenty thousand," said Dawley. "I don't believe I can do anything for you, Hammond."

"You mean you won't renew?" gasped the other.

"Exactly that."

Hammond's eyes grew wide, his face paled, his hands gripped the arms of his chair hard.

"Why, good God, man, that will bust me wide open!"

"Sorry." Dawley's gaze was expressionless. His only emotion was that of curiosity to see how Hammond was taking it. "You got that loan from William Burgess. He let you have it on the strength of some copper you discovered on your property. Well, copper doesn't amount to much in this country unless you have a railroad to haul it. And the new railroad isn't coming through Paro. Your mine is practically worthless. The Burgess estate needs money. That's all, Hammond."

He sat watching Hammond as the latter got to his feet and started for the door.

Later, Dawley went to the courthouse.

"Issue an order of foreclosure against Jay Hammond," he instructed. "For twenty thousand dollars, with interest, in favor of the Burgess estate. Name Coleman appraiser. I'll tell him the figures."

"You'll buy it in at auction, I suppose?" suggested Judge Quinn.

"Certainly," laughed Dawley. "It is perfectly legitimate, isn't it?"

"Perfectly." The judge was sarcastic. "God, man, but you are ruthless. Why not give Hammond a chance?"

"I am not a philanthropist," jeered Dawley. "Too many men of Paro have pinned their faith to the prospect of the new railroad coming through here. Have Mogridge serve the papers today, Quinn."

Dawley went back to the bank, and for a long time conferred with Glenmere. At noon he lunched at the City Hotel. Coming out, he found Mogridge awaiting him.

"I've served the papers on Hammond," he told Dawley. "He's in the High Card lickin' up forty-rod, an' killin' mad! Look out!"

"Thanks." Dawley smiled at Mogridge as he crossed the street and entered the bank. An hour later Hammond burst in through the front door.

The man had been drinking. There was a six-shooter in his right hand, his muscles were twitching, his eyes blazing. He had lost his self-control, and there was murder in his heart.

"Here you are, eh?" he sneered harshly. "You damned cheap crook! Wouldn't renew my note! Gamblin' with Bill Burgess' money—runnin' fast an' loose with it! They've been tellin' me how you work it! Foreclose on me, force a sale on Burgess' holdin's an' buy in with your own money, eh? For a song! I'm goin' to salivate you—sure as hell!"

"You're drunk, Hammond," said Dawley quietly. Then unhesitatingly he took three or four steps toward Hammond, Hammond watching him with a sort of stupidness that came from wonder over the absolute fearlessness of the other in advancing upon a loaded revolver. Tardily Hammond saw the cold, implacable resolution in Dawley's eyes; the icy, calculating glint that should have warned him.

Dawley's tigerlike leap caught Hammond off guard, even though he had been prepared for something of the kind—having heard tales of the man's coolness. Resistlessly Hammond was flung back against the door jamb; his body turned slightly sidewise so that he could not bring the pistol to bear on the other man.

Dawley's weight, as he catapulted against Hammond, crushed the breath out of the other, staggered him. And before Hammond could stiffen his muscles his pistol arm was seized in a grip that made him wince. Holding Hammond with the weight of his own body, Dawley slipped his hand upward on the other's arm until his fingers closed over the stock of the pistol. Hammond's arm was pushed upward until the muzzle of the pistol pointed outward through the open doorway. Then Dawley's finger pressed savagely upon Hammond's where the latter's rested on the trigger, and the weapon exploded six times, the bullets flying harmlessly over the tops of Paro's buildings.

Then, before Hammond had time to recover from his surprise, his right arm was wrenched and twisted until the pistol dropped from his hand. Still crushed against the door jamb, Hammond began to fight back. His efforts were vain. Dawley's iron fingers fastened themselves upon Hammond's throat.

Hammond wrenched and squirmed, kicking and threshing in an effort to tear himself free. Coldly and apparently without emotion, and with much the same expression in his eyes that had been there when he had looked across the table at Hammond, Dawley increased the pressure of his fingers.

When Hammond's face began to turn black and his body became limp, Dawley released his grip, swung the man in his arms, carried him into the street and dropped him into the dust.

Late that night, returning from the Dawley Dance Hall, Dawley received news that made an impression upon his cold composure.

Two horsemen on tired, dusty ponies awaited him in the street. One, leaning against a corner of a building, was weak from loss of blood and cursing softly from the pain of two wounds in the shoulder. The other, with a bandaged hand which he tenderly touched as he talked, sat crosswise in the saddle.

"Joe and Pete!" snapped Dawley. "What's wrong?"

"He's come!" groaned Pete. "We laid for him at Spring dugout—as you told us to do. We tried to nail him, an' missed. Then he done some shootin' on his own account. He played with us, damn him! Chased us, plug gin' us, an' laffin' at us!"

Dawley cursed the men, telling them to get away, quick, or he'd finish the job their intended victim had neglected.

Dawley went to his rooms above the bank. He got into bed, but could not sleep. A little later, sitting in a chair at a little distance back from one of the front windows, he saw a horseman loping his animal toward the City Hotel. He peered forward, watching intently.

The horseman made his way leisurely through the ankle-deep dust of the street toward the hotel. When he reached a point in front of the bank building he drew the horse to a halt, and for some time sat motionless in the saddle, looking at the building. To Dawley, watching with a sullen, malevolent glare, it seemed that the horseman's attitude was that of a penitent.

Dawley grinned mirthlessly. He saw the horseman dismount and go into the hotel. Later he came out and looked again toward the bank. There was something in his attitude this time—a suggestion of confidence, a poise that hinted of a knowledge and trust of self that aroused a cold antagonism in Dawley's soul. He sneered, but a chill of dire premonition swept over him as he sought his bed.

CHAPTER FOUR

By morning Dawley had conquered the premonition of evil, and he laughed shortly as he dressed and descended to the street. He went to Judge Quinn's house and got him up.

"Clay Burgess is in town, Quinn," he said evenly.

The judge gasped, and a pulse of anxiety seized him.

"I told you not to do it, Dawley! Those things always bring trouble."

"Told me not to do what?" glowered Dawley. "Talk, you damned fool!"

"That will you made me record," blurted the judge. "I told you not to do it!"

"Bah!" Dawley's voice snapped with savage contempt. "Have you looked at it lately? Look at it, then. When Ben Davis left here he left his notary seal in his office, to be returned to the governor. Ben Davis' seal and signature are on the will you recorded."

"You placed them there?" The judge gulped over this fresh evidence of Dawley's crookedness.

"H-m," grunted Dawley derisively.

"Suppose Davis should return?"

"Look here," said Dawley, ignoring the question. "If I'm not mistaken, there's going to be hell to pay with this man Burgess. There can't be any namby-pamby business going on in the courthouse—understand? You are the judge of the court here, and the governor is behind you in everything you do. And he'll be against you if you try to run in any ranikaboo on me. I'm going to have a talk with Burgess in your court some time today—if Burgess forces my hand—and I want you to be on the job right along. Mogridge and Coleman will be hanging around all day. You are not to let Burgess bullyrag you for a minute. Understand? I just came to warn you. That's all."

Dawley left the judge and routed out the sheriff, with whom he had a long talk. Then Dawley found Dal Coleman.

Dawley talked long with Coleman, and the latter grinned slyly when Dawley took leave of him. Then Dawley went to the hotel, breakfasted, and lingered for a few minutes to talk with the clerk. Then he went to the bank and shut himself in.

Clay Burgess was early astir. He bore no marks of the meeting with Dawley's two men the night before. He had mentally catalogued them as ordinary holdup men.

Shortly after dawn he fed his horse. Going in to breakfast he missed Dawley by a matter of minutes.

At the desk, after breakfast, he discovered, through the clerk, that his father was dead. Except for a quick whitening of the lips he gave no sign of how the news had shocked him. He made some inquiries, and then mounted Darkey and rode away toward the Bar B, the ranch upon which he had spent his boyhood days.

Some time after leaving Paro he stood on the side of a hill where there were several headboards, with the earth conventionally mounded around them. He lingered long near one, looking at the crude lettering upon it, his eyes misty, his lips set queerly.

"I'm sorry, dad," he said finally. "I'd like to make it up to you."

Later he rode several miles to a group of buildings in a little basin near a river. He did not go near the house, but he noted men and cattle at a distance, and so he knew that someone was working the property. It was nearly noon when he returned to

Paro, and he halted Darkey in front of the bank building and dismounted.

A moment later Burgess was standing in the doorway of the directors' room, looking at Dawley.

Dawley pretended to be interested in some papers on his desk, and with his wide-brimmed hat dangling from his hand Burgess deferentially waited. Dawley turned at last, smiling smoothly.

"Well, sir?"

"I am Clay Burgess, son of William Burgess," said the other, lowly and politely.

He leaned forward a little, in anticipation of the welcoming hand that he expected Dawley would reach out to him. He was ready to thank Dawley for looking after the Burgess property during his absence.

The hand was not extended. Dawley's face was cold and emotionless. He did not even wave Burgess to a chair, but sat, leaning slightly back in his own, regarding Burgess with a slight squint of doubt.

"Clay Burgess, eh?" he said slowly. "It seems, now that you mention it, that Burgess *did* remark once that he had a son—somewhere. You—if you *are* his son—did not get along well with your father?"

Burgess flushed. The tone used by the other was insinuatingly patronizing and freighted with a hint of sarcasm. For the first time since reaching the doorway Burgess gazed appraisingly at the other. Dawley met the gaze and returned it, and for a space no word was spoken.

They were valuing each other, searching, probing for good and evil, each trying to test the mental strength of the other. Both were alert for weaknesses, both aware that nothing could come of the exchange except a strengthening of the antagonism that had been aroused by Dawley's attitude.

Dawley's eyes wavered at last. "Well?" he snapped.

"I am William Burgess' son, Clay. I have been—somewhere. Just where, is my business. I got along well with my father. I'll get along better with you if you talk straight." Burgess put his hat on his head and folded his arms. "Let's get to an understanding," he said shortly. "What are you doing in the Burgess bank?"

"I'm managing this bank. I am also managing the other property of the Burgess estate. I am the executor, regularly appointed by the court here."

"For how long?"

"Until the legal heir appears and is duly identified and qualified."

Burgess smiled.

"All right, Mr. Dawley. I shall relieve you of your duties as quickly as possible."

He turned his back to Dawley, leaving the door open behind him, went out, and made his way to the courthouse. Shortly, he was standing in front of the desk behind which sat Judge Quinn.

"I'm Clay Burgess, son of William Burgess," he announced quietly. "I petition the court to recognize me as the heir of William Burgess. I also ask for the discharge of a man named Dawley as executor."

The judge looked up at him, his face a trifle white, his eyes furtive.

"Certainly," he said. "If you are the Burgess heir the court will be glad to turn the property over to you. But, of course, you will have to be properly identified—to my satisfaction. That is, to the satisfaction of the court. I shall summon Mr. Dawley. He was rather intimate with your father, and no doubt he will be able to aid in the identification and settle matters immediately."

Judge Quinn was nervous, his hands were trembling. The presence in the court all morning of Sheriff Mogridge and Dal Coleman had contributed nothing to Quinn's peace of mind. He would have given much to have been able to rule the courtroom as he knew it should be ruled, but the inexorable will of Dawley was master of his, and though he sensed an undercurrent of subtle preparation in the events of the morning, and particularly in the significance of the presence of Mogridge and Coleman, he had not the moral courage to discourage it.

He looked at Coleman, who sat in a corner behind the judge's desk, taking a sidelong glance at him. Coleman was lounging in his chair, his right side toward the desk where Burgess was standing, and the judge shivered when he noted that the stock of the man's pistol seemed to be very convenient to his right hand.

Mogridge, too, was in a lounging attitude, and his right hand was hanging carelessly over the arm of his chair, the drooping fingers caressing, with seeming abstractedness, the butt of his six-shooter.

The judge cleared his throat as he took a final glance at Mogridge.

"Mogridge," he said, "go down to the bank and tell Dawley to come here."

"Dawley is here, your honor." The executor stood in the open doorway smiling. He stepped in, closing the door behind him.

The judge coughed. "I suggested that perhaps you might be able to vouch for this man's identity."

"He *claims* to be Clay Burgess," smiled Dawley.

Burgess laughed. "I can appreciate your predicament, your honor. Also my own. Personally, I am satisfied that I am Clay Burgess, and my job is to convince you that I am. That is not so easy as it appears to be, is it? I never, thought of the matter in that light. Would you be satisfied if I were to call in someone who is personally known to you—who would be willing to swear to my identity?"

The judge glanced quickly at Dawley, but the latter was looking at Coleman.

"Why, y-yes," agreed the judge.

Burgess' face grew thoughtful, then it reddened, for only one name, of all those that he had been familiar with in the old days, had remained fixed in his memory.

"I could get Ben Davis," he said.

"Very likely," laughed Dawley derisively. "Only Ben Davis is not here any more. He left Paro some time ago—between days. Nobody knows where he went. Try again."

"Bill Harding?" suggested Burgess, the memory of another old acquaintance assailing him.

"Died four years ago," offered Dawley.

"Legget?" Burgess' memory was beginning to become refreshed.

"I bought him out seven years ago," said Dawley. "He left the country shortly afterward."

"Harvey Dobble?" suggested Burgess.

Dawley changed color. But he stepped forward, smiling blandly.

"You were rather abrupt to me a while ago—at the bank. We'll let that pass. I take it you didn't like my looks—and I don't like you. I tell you that frankly. But to show you that I never let my personal feelings interfere in a matter of this kind I shall try to help you out.

"I've heard William Burgess say that his son Clay bears a scar on his right shoulder near the center of the back. It was made by three rowel points of a Mexican spur, by a greaser who was angered at young Burgess for some reason, and who kicked at him. It is improbable that two persons should bear the same sort of scar, and I have no doubt that if you are able to show such a scar to Judge Quinn he will be satisfied as to your identity."

Burgess was smiling now, and his eyes were alight with satisfaction.

"I bear the mark, your honor," he said to the judge; and he thanked Dawley.

The latter smiled coldly, and, turning faced Coleman, at whom he deliberately winked.

Burgess was already removing his shirt. Unbuckling his cartridge belt, he laid belt and pistols on the desk beside Judge Quinn. After pulling his shirt over his head, he stood, naked to the waist, and turned his back to the judge. Three ragged-looking marks, which evidently had been made in the manner described by Dawley, appeared on the right shoulderblade.

"That seems to be satisfactory," acknowledged the judge.

Mogridge got to his feet, clearing his throat, and sauntered toward Burgess.

"That's a queer place for a fellow to get jabbed," he remarked. "Got any objections to me takin' a look at it?"

Burgess walked toward him. Mogridge turned Burgess around so that he stood between Burgess and the desk. He looked at the scars, and remarked:

"They're there, all right," and with his left hand shoved Burgess from him violently, drawing a pistol as he did so. When Burgess turned swiftly, his eyes flashing resentfully, he looked fairly into the muzzle of the sheriff's pistol.

"Keep standin'!" warned the sheriff sharply. "You make one move toward them guns on the desk an' I bore you plenty. There's a guy wearin' three scars like that wanted for tryin' to salivate two guys at Spring dugout, on the Star range!"

Burgess stiffened. After the first flash of surprise his face showed his deep disgust over the easy manner in which Dawley had fooled him.

Two things that seemed mysterious to him were now perfectly clear. The first of these was Dawley's suggestion about the scars. But any man might have been misled by that. Second, there was the attack by the two holdup men the night before, when he had been approaching Paro.

Dawley wanted him killed, and had set the two men upon him. The fact that Dawley had connived with Mogridge to get him to set his pistols aside, so that the sheriff could arrest him, indicated that. He might have known as soon as Dawley had exhibited antagonism toward him in the bank that Dawley was the man who wanted him killed. That had been his own fault.

He glanced swiftly around him. A sinister silence had descended upon the room. Judge Quinn was not in the plot. Burgess was certain of that—or the judge was a weak tool in the hands of the master plotter, Dawley.

Burgess studied the faces of the others rapidly. They meant murder; that was apparent. It was in their faces. In front of him, Mogridge's body was in a crouch, and his eyes were narrowed with cold resolution. Burgess knew that with his slightest movement Mogridge would pull the trigger of his weapon.

Coleman, too, had got to his feet. He had shifted forward until he stood within ten paces of the sheriff. A six-shooter was in his right hand. Like the sheriff, he was crouching.

"Plug him if he moves an eyelash, Mogridge!" Dawley ordered. " 'Slow' Burgess, eh?" he jeered. "You came here, unannounced to take right hold of things. Bah! I've had a man dogging you for six months. Slow? Well, I reckon you're some slow! Mogridge is going to blow you apart for resisting arrest! Get that? Let him have it, Mogridge!"

Burgess had considered his chances while Dawley had been speaking—and before. While Dawley was mouthing his last venomous words Burgess was estimating the distance that separated him from Mogridge. Before the order to shoot had left Dawley's lips Burgess had made the leap he had meditated.

The flame-spurt from the sheriff's pistol passed under Burgess' arm while his body was in the air. The left arm went around Mogridge's neck as Burgess' feet struck the floor. It was contracted rigidly, with a violence that snapped the sheriff's head back as though it were on a hinge. Burgess slipped behind him with the movement, swinging him around so that his body would make a shield for any bullets that might come from Coleman.

Dawley had drawn no weapon. With the disarrangement of his plans he was bawling orders to Coleman, blasphemous and bitter. Coleman, his mouth working soundlessly, was working his way around toward the wall, trying to get to one side of Burgess and the helpless sheriff so that he would have a better target. Burgess was forcing the sheriff backward in order to get him nearer the pistols on the judge's desk.

Conscious of the danger of the situation and of his fault in not being prepared for Burgess' leap, Mogridge was cursing savagely as he tried to squirm out of his captor's grasp. His efforts met with failure, for the arm around his neck was like a slowly constricting bar of iron that threatened to shut off his breath. Mogridge kept his right arm extended, being conscious of the efforts of Burgess to secure it.

And that was Burgess' aim. Inch by inch, like a bulldog at the throat of an enemy, he slid his grip toward the sheriff's hand. With Burgess' fingers sinking into his forearm Mogridge fought desperately. But the arm was dragged back, and with a rapid shift Burgess slid his hand downward still farther until it closed on the sheriff's hand.

There was a final struggle, and then the sheriff's arm swung around until the muzzle of his weapon in his hand was directed at Coleman. Mogridge cursed as he was forced to pull the trigger, but as the pistol exploded and Coleman pitched forward, face down on the floor, Mogridge wrenched himself free, the pistol still in hand. He tried to wheel around to face Burgess, and did throw one shot at him, backward, as he turned. But before he could twist all the way around Burgess struck him bitterly at the back of the ear with his fist, sending him reeling.

Burgess had worked with a savage energy that made his movements too rapid for the eye to follow. And when Mogridge went staggering from him, and he turned to leap to the judge's desk for his pistols, Dawley, disconcerted by the rapidity of Burgess' movements, was just beginning to realize that he might fail. But he noted Burgess' leap toward the two pistols on the desk, and he sprang forward, grunting venomously, in an effort to balk him.

They met just in front of the desk with a shock that seemed to jar the building. Their arms went around each other's necks as they instinctively fought for wrestlers' holds. Reeling from the force of the first impact, they crashed into some chairs at one side of the desk, and Dawley, the one to be caught off balance, tripped over them and went down into the wreck, Burgess on top of him.

Dawley, in a demoniac rage over the miscarriage of his plans, fought furiously. Normally strong, his rage gave him added strength, and he threshed about in the wreck of the chairs until, getting an advantageous hold, he began to turn Burgess over.

The latter resisted, but Dawley succeeded partially in his design, rolling Burgess entirely off so that the two lay on the floor, clear of the chairs, Burgess on his left side, Dawley on his right, locked tightly in each other's arms, their faces together.

Dawley's arms—one of them under Burgess' left arm and across his back, the fingers twisted into the waistband of the other's chaps, where they were fastened at the hips; the other under Burgess' right arm and bent forward over the right shoulder, with the palm of the hand under Burgess' chin—were rigid as steel bands. Burgess' right arm was almost helpless; it stuck up in the air like a distress signal, waving eccentrically as its owner tried to wriggle it out of the enemy's clutch.

Burgess' left arm, though, was working terrible execution. In spite of the terrific pressure Dawley was exerting with the palm of the hand under Burgess' chin—forcing the chin back always, and shutting off Burgess' breath, Burgess kept his left arm working with deadly precision and crushing force into Dawley's face.

Dawley twisted his head here and there to escape the terrific hammering. Unable to evade the punishment, he loosed the grip of his right hand and snapped his head backward. The movement cost him what little advantage he had, for instantly Burgess writhed free of the other hand and lunged forward, throwing a leg over Dawley and rolling on top of him.

Anticipating that movement at its inception, Dawley added impetus to it, continuing to roll when Burgess landed on top of him. They went over and over, missing the desk by inches, tightly locked together, fighting silently and furiously.

Beyond the desk they broke free for an instant, and as though by mutual arrangement they scrambled to their feet. For an instant after rising they stood and glared at each other, and then Dawley, his face malignant, bruised and macerated in half a dozen places where Burgess' fists had landed, lunged forward, making a hideous grimace, driving a fist at Burgess' face.

Burgess slipped the blow, stepping lightly aside like a boxer, and as Dawley went past him, reeling from the wasted effort, Burgess caught him under the chin with a vicious, deadening uppercut.

The blow stunned Dawley. His knees sagged, his head wobbled, and he stood with glazing eyes, his hands hanging helplessly at his sides. Tensing himself for a final blow, Burgess again launched himself at his enemy.

Sensing movement behind him, he halted, wheeling like a flash. Mogridge was standing not more than three or four paces from him, in the act of leveling his gun.

Burgess' wheeling movement was continuous and accomplished with the swiftness of light. Not being near enough to strike with his fist, he swung his left foot upward, aiming for the weapon in the sheriff's hand. The toe of the boot missed the pistol, passing it and landing under the sheriff's chin with a queer, sudden crash.

But just the instant before the boot landed, Mogridge pulled the trigger. Burgess felt the powder sting his face; a sharp, agonizing pain shot through his left shoulder; the arm dropped helplessly to his side.

Mogridge went down like a log. Burgess saw Dawley not more than a dozen paces from him, making his way toward the pistols on the judge's desk. Burgess reached them while Dawley was still several paces away. He snatched one from its holster.

Dawley waited. He had recovered from the blow, and he stood perfectly still as Burgess looked at him. He realized that if he moved, Burgess would kill him.

For an instant it seemed that the passion that gripped Burgess would drive him to shoot Dawley—and Dawley stiffened, watching with sullen, wondering, and sneering gaze.

Burgess did not shoot. He grinned with cold contempt at Dawley. He deliberately laid the naked pistol on the desk beside him, and painfully put on shirt and cartridge belt.

"Slow—eh?" he jeered at Dawley. "Well, I reckon I'm fast enough."

He turned to the judge, who was cringing in his chair.

"You saw what happened," he said. He was breathing fast. He made a menacing picture with the pistol in hand.

But the judge looked past him at Dawley.

"It was a frame-up!" said Burgess to the judge. "You know that! You—"

"He killed Coleman," interposed Dawley hoarsely. "Order his arrest!"

"Yes—you shot Coleman. I—I saw it." The judge raised his voice now, and Burgess saw that many faces were at the windows.

"I call upon the people of this town to arrest this man!" shouted the judge. "He has killed Coleman, and maybe the sheriff! Arrest him!"

"So you're crooked, too!" said Burgess.

He was grinning bitterly, and his voice came with a sharp, metallic snap. He swung around, backing toward the door, his pistol sweeping the faces at the windows, the judge, and Dawley.

"Everybody stand!" he ordered. "I down the first man that moves a finger!"

CHAPTER FIVE

Still backing, Burgess reached the door and flung it open. For an instant he stood framed in the opening, sweeping the attentive crowd with cold, alert glances.

Nobody moved. Still backing away, still menacing them all with the pistol, Burgess reached Darkey. With a quick leap he was in the saddle, and before his feet could find the stirrups the black horse was thundering down the street, his flying hoofs sending the dust splaying in all directions.

"Go after him!" bawled Dawley from the doorway.

Derisive grins greeted Dawley's words. A man far back in the crowd guffawed loudly:

"It's your game, mister man. Play it yourself!"

For a distance of two or three miles the black horse held a rapid pace, covering the ground with long, swift, leaping strides. Then, scanning the back trail and seeing no signs of pursuit, Burgess drew the black down and gave some attention to the wound in his shoulder.

The bullet had gone clear through him, rather high, paralyzing the big muscles of the arm and shoulder. He could feel the shirt sticking to his back, and knew that the wound must have bled much there, while in front he was drenched—a patch on the grey shirt grew larger as he watched it.

There was nothing he could do except to attempt to stop the bleeding. Taking his handkerchief from a pocket, he stuffed it between the shirt and the wound. Then, speaking to Darkey, he sent him forward, following a narrow trail that led eastward.

He faintly remembered the trail as one he had ridden years before. It led to a section of broken country just beyond the big level where he was riding. He seemed to have recollections of a waterhole near the edge of the broken country. If it were still there, he could stop and tend to the wound, and then he could ride northeastward to Fillets, over the county line, where he could stay until the wound healed. Later he would return to Paro to square his account with Judge Quinn, Dawley, and Mogridge.

He had no delusions regarding his chance of securing fair treatment at Paro. He had no plans for the future beyond a determination to even the score with Dawley. Uppermost in his mind was a realization of the necessity of getting somewhere quickly, that his wound might receive the attention it needed.

He was beginning to feel a gradual waning of strength. Unmistakably his right hand trembled, and he felt himself swaying slightly from side to side. At first the movement was barely noticeable, but as he continued to ride forward and the swaying grew more pronounced, he halted Darkey and with a grin of grim derision took note of the movement. He had been hurt more badly than he had thought. Objects were swimming in his vision. He fixed his gaze on a clump of filmy mesquite dead ahead on the trail, and was surprised to see it dipping grotesquely.

The derision on his face faded and was succeeded by a frown. A bitter, vicious rage seized him, and for an instant he meditated returning to Paro to send Dawley and Mogridge ahead of him to that death which he was now certain he was going to meet.

He swung Darkey around, heading him toward Paro. Then a thought of his condition dissuaded him. For in that direction lay more fighting, and he was in no shape to meet it. If he kept on toward Fillets there was a chance for him.

Abruptly wheeling Darkey, he sent him forward again. For an hour he rode steadily, the reins hanging from the pommel of the saddle, his right hand pressed against the neckerchief over the wound.

The swaying of his body had grown more noticeable. Indeed there were several times during the next hour when he did not know whether he was riding at all, or whether he was even moving. After a great while he became vaguely aware that Darkey had halted. With an effort he steadied himself and gazed around him, fixing objects in his vision with a sort of wearied concentration.

Almost at Darkey's feet he saw the water he had set out to seek. He feebly patted Darkey's mane, and slipped out of the saddle, falling into the sun-dried mud that surrounded the water, and, reaching blindly outward, trying to touch it with his hands.

Burgess had no means of knowing how long he had been unconscious, nor was he convinced—after a long period of serious consideration—that he *now* was conscious. For the scene upon which he opened his eyes seemed to be as unreal as the other fantasies with which his brain had struggled through an interminable time. So, after taking one look at his surroundings, he closed his eyes.

He had seen a log-ribbed ceiling, a roof, evidently. Next his perplexed eyes had observed a window close to his side, with a white muslin curtain fluttering in a slight breeze.

Then his gaze roved to the walls, where he saw shelves upon which were pictures and other ornaments. The pictures were small, and the other decorations not pretentious or valuable, but the presence of wall decorations, added to the undoubted fact of a muslin curtain at a window, suggested the presence of a woman—and Burgess was convinced that he was not dreaming. Then he turned his head slightly and saw her. At which he closed his eyes and smiled in faint self-derision.

After a time he again opened his eyes. She was sitting near an open door, busy with a needle, and her gaze was upon the open country that she was facing.

He must have gone to sleep again, for when next he saw the girl she was moving about in the room, from a stove to a table, and the aroma of cooking things assailed Burgess. She had donned an apron, and looked toward him.

"Awake?" she said.

"I don't know. I've been trying to figure it out. I've been doing considerable dreaming, I reckon. But I don't seem to be able to work *you* in anywhere. Don't tell me that presently you'll go flitting away like—like a lot of other people that I've been talking to lately."

"I never 'flit,' " she said. "You mustn't talk—much. You have been terribly hurt, and we have had quite a time getting you over it. If there is anything you want to know, I shall be glad to do what I can. But you positively must not talk."

"All right," he grinned. "I'll listen. I remember being shot—in Paro. Then I started my horse—where is he, please?" he broke off anxiously.

"In the corral. Ben has been taking good care of him."

"I started my horse toward a waterhole, which I thought I knew. That's all I remember. What happened then?"

"You reached the waterhole. It was late in the afternoon of the day before yesterday. Ben had gone away. I ran out of water and had to go for it myself. I saw you lying there. Your face was in the water near the edge. I—I am afraid I was scared. But I took care of your wound, gave you some water, and got you here—before Ben came."

"How?"

"I can hardly tell you. Your horse helped. He is a wonderful animal. I got him to lie down, and I got you across him. Then he got up and carried you—oh, so carefully! Then Ben came, and we worked almost all night over you."

"Who is Ben?"

"Ben is—Ben Davis. He used to be justice of the peace in Paro—until Dave Dawley forced him to leave. He was my father's friend."

Burgess gritted his teeth in his delight, for he knew Davis.

The girl continued. "Ben Davis was therefore compelled to settle here."

"Where is 'here'?" he asked.

" 'Here' is a little cabin about half a mile from the waterhole you thought you remembered. It is about eighteen miles from Paro, and five miles from Williams' cache. We call Williams' cache Dawley's camp."

"Why?"

"Dawley is ruthless. He has broken a number of men. He rules Paro. He is the law and the law's prophet. If a man gets in his way he outlaws him. He is implacable. Most of the men he has broken are in Williams' cache. It is a stretch of unsurveyed and unclaimed land not yet legally attached to any state or territory. Not even a governor's power reaches there. Extradition is unhead of. At least Mogridge's kind do not attempt to go there.

"Not all of Dawley's camp is composed of men sent there by Dawley. It is a rendezvous for criminals of all descriptions. 'Flash' Denby is the ruler of the cache. I never heard his real name. They call him Flash because he is the quickest gunman in the country."

She must have divined from the expression of his face that he was wondering why she lived so close to a place of such ill-repute, for she raised her chin and looked at him with flashing, resolute eyes.

"They do not molest me," she said with conscious pride. "Twice they tried to, but they were eager to get away. You see," she smiled, "I was born and raised in Wyoming, where I learned to do a number of things that young women who live in more settled communities never hear of. When my father lost his ranch in Wyoming because he shot a man for stealing his cattle, we lost everything. I was in school at the time—in California—and daddy came here without me. My mother died before that. I came here with daddy—after a while. My father was Elam Bowen, and I am Della Bowen."

Burgess had heard of the incident prominent in the annals of cattle-raising in Wyoming, referred to as the "Bowen war," and he looked with a new interest at the daughter of the man who had fought a manly, courageous fight against mighty odds—to lose when the machinery of a law manipulated in the interests of unscrupulous men had centered its power against him. He drew a breath of admiration and sympathy.

"Your father found nothing here, I reckon?"

"Copper!" she breathed, her eyes gleaming with enthusiasm. "Tons and tons and tons of it! Free ore in chunks as big as your hand. Rotted and crumbling on the surface, waiting for someone to take it—waiting there for ages, six inches under the ground! I'll show it to you some day."

"And no railroad nearer than Taos," reminded Burgess gently.

"No," she said, her enthusiasm waning. "Much as there is of it, it wouldn't pay to haul it that far."

"Eighty miles, eh? And it's a rough trail."

Clay briefly told of his quarrel with Dawley, and how the latter had secured possession of the Burgess estate.

The girl flushed. "Our property, too, is in Dawley's clutches."
His eyes gleamed.

"How did he happen to get hold of it?"

"Father was penniless when he came here. Your father grub-staked him. But Dawley has taken charge. Oh, why didn't you kill him!" she breathed savagely.

"I reckon I don't know. I think it was because shooting wouldn't satisfy me. I don't see how my father grubstaking your dad lets Dawley in on the property."

She told him the things Ben Davis had acquainted her with, regarding Dawley's management of the estate. When she concluded, Burgess laughed lowly.

"It's pretty plain, I reckon. Dawley wants to get control of all the copper. But with no railroad nearer than Taos—"

"There has been talk of the railroad coming through Paro." She saw him scowl. "They have almost reached Dry Bottom, coming this way. No one—except Dawley, perhaps—knows where the road is going after leaving Dry Bottom."

"Dawley knows," he said. "It's a big steal. Most likely the governor is interested in it."

He lay quiet for a time, looking out of the window, she watching him narrowly, anxiously.

"And," she said after a time, "you can't do anything. I can do nothing. As yet Dawley hasn't bothered me. He hasn't even been over here. But when he turns his attention to us—to Davis and me—we shall have to get out. For I haven't the money to clear the place. And you," she added, with a strange, wistful look at him, "you have outlawed yourself. Dal Coleman is dead. Mogridge, Dawley, and Judge Quinn declare you killed him. You dare not return to Paro—they would hang you."

He laughed lowly, turning his head to look at her, a slow, ironic grin on his face.

"It can't be Elam Bowen's daughter that I hear saying she can't do anything," he said. "It must be that I'm still dreaming. I knew all along I was dreaming, but I kept hoping and hoping. Well, so long, ma'am. I've sure enjoyed your company, but I'll go to sleep again, and maybe I'll wake up and find that it's all a mistake. Maybe I'll find that Elam Bowen's daughter has changed her mind—if you're sure her—and that she's going to fight Dawley and Mogridge and Judge Quinn and the governor, and anyone else that tries to take her belongings from her. And maybe she'll find some consolation in knowing she's going to have company in that kind of a fight. You might tell her that a guy named Clay Burgess is going to do a lot of scrapping himself one of these days—when he's had enough sleep and mountains of grub to eat—and when Elam's daughter says she's with him."

"I am!" she whispered, coming close to him. "Oh, I am so glad! I was afraid—" she paused, and blushed.

"Afraid of what?"

"Afraid that you wouldn't—wouldn't be—what Ben Davis said he wanted you to be—what he hoped you'd be—what you are—a fighter!"

"Fighter!" he laughed joyously. "Why, I'm whipped right now!" And he turned his face from her—she noted a flush on it—leaving her to speculate upon his meaning.

CHAPTER SIX

For seven weeks, while Burgess' wound knitted and the glow of health came back into his face, there was a lull in the intense action that had followed Burgess' arrival at Paro City. No word came from the town, except through the medium of Ben Davis' friend, Harvey Dobble, owner of the general store and a pioneer who had come to Paro before Dawley's time, and who did not like the man.

Paro was quiet, Dobble said. Apparently Dawley and Mogridge were satisfied that Burgess had left the town never to return, for they seemed to have lost all interest in him. That, at least, was the surface indication.

Burgess grinned to Davis after Dobble's visit.

"I've been doing a lot of thinking, Ben."

Davis' keen old eyes glinted with savage scorn.

"What you intendin' to do?"

"About Dawley? What would you suggest?" There was a gleam of amusement in Burgess' eyes. He and Davis had pursued this subject before, without reaching a conclusion.

"You're always comin' back to me with that there damned wise question!" snapped Davis. He glared at the other in futile rage. "I ain't no damned plotter like Dawley, or mebbe I could frame up somethin'. There's your dad's will, that I've showed you. There's Dawley, skinnin' you out of your property every day you set here doin' nothin'. What are you goin' to do about it?"

"Nothing, now." Burgess looked gravely at the grim face of the other. "What's the use of getting excited about it? Dawley will steal everything he can get his hands on, I reckon. But he can't steal Dave Dawley. And as long as Dawley stays in the country I'm not afraid of him getting away from me."

"Dobble sneaked a look at the record book in the courthouse the other day," said Davis. "He saw an item in there, reading that your dad had willed all his property to Dawley in case you didn't show up an' qualify for it. That there clause makes it mighty profitable for Dawley to plug you promiscuous—him grabbin' off everything after you've cashed in."

"That ought to spur Dawley to action," smiled Burgess.

"An' you, too, durn you! If I was you I'd slip into Paro an' salivate the whole damned crew—Dawley, Mogridge, an' that cringin' crook of a judge!"

"But being Ben Davis, you can only give bad advice to a lazy and worthless fellow named Clay Burgess."

"Well," said Davis, disgusted surrender in his eyes and voice, "I reckon you'll have your way about it—whatever that way is. The guy that tacked the handle 'Slow' on you sure must have seen you when your brain-box was crammed full of worthless thoughts—or a woman. You'll get a-goin' some time, I reckon. But if I was your dad I'd wallop you till the fur would fly! Bein' only Ben Davis, your dad's old side-kicker, I can only set back proud an' scornful, cogitatin' on why men don't make a better job of it in raisin' their sons. I reckon that little fracas you had in the courthouse with Dawley an' Coleman an' Mogridge was a whizzer. It wouldn't have come off if Dawley hadn't forced your hand. You ain't got gumption enough to start nothin' yourself!"

Burgess chuckled as he watched Davis stamp away toward the stable, muttering wrathfully. Burgess was still smiling over the old man's impatience when a little later he stepped inside the cabin door and drank from a dipper that hung on the wall over a pail of water.

"Thank you, ma'am," he said gravely and earnestly to Della. "Thank you for seven weeks of tending me like an angel. Well, so-long, ma'am," he added. "I reckon I can be going now."

She stepped swiftly to the doorway and stood in it, looking at him, startled over the abruptness of his leave-taking, a shade of anxiety in her eyes.

"Where are you going?" she asked.

"To Williams' cache, ma'am." He grinned hugely. "I'm going to be a simon-pure outlaw now, ma'am. And may-be I'm wasting my time, after all."

"Oh!" she said. "You mustn't go there!"

"Do you want Ben Davis to be saying that I haven't got gumption enough to start anything? Do you think I want him to go telling you that? He told me this morning!"

"Well, then—if you are determined to go—I suppose you will. But—" She paused, and he saw a light in her eyes that made him draw a slow, deep breath.

He waved a hand to her from the corral, where he saddled the black horse and swung into the saddle. Again, from the big level near the house as he rode northeastward, he waved to her, and she stood on the threshold of the door answering his signals until he and the black horse, traveling in a dust cloud, vanished in a distant depression.

She was still standing on the threshold half an hour later when Ben Davis, back from a ride in the hills, came upon her.

"Burgess has gone," she told him, her face a trifle pale, her lips stiff.

"Gone!" exclaimed Davis. "Gone where?"

"To Williams' cache," she told him. "He said that, henceforth, he intended to be an outlaw—a Dawley out-law."

"The durn fool!" grumbled Davis. "I knowed damn' well he'd go an' start somethin'!"

When leaving Paro City some weeks before, Burgess had given no thought to the future. He had been able to think of no plan for revenge upon the smooth-talking, deep-thinking enemy who had, during the first day of his stay in Paro, enmeshed him in a carefully laid plot. His thoughts, when he had left Paro behind him, were in a turmoil of impotent rage. Only one thing was definite—that one day he would square things with Dawley. Yet he had known that the possibility was remote, for he could not return to Paro openly.

But during the days of his convalescence, through the long, lingering, and peaceful hours when he had lain on his back looking out of the window, and during other hours—afterward—when he had been able to make his way outdoors, he had meditated much upon the situation, and had finally evolved a plan of action that—if it did not miscarry—would make the future very interesting for Dawley.

Every man's actions are governed by his estimate of himself. Burgess did not make the mistake of valuing himself too highly. There was a vein of grim humor in the mental makeup that governed him. It was that grim humor which was sending Burgess to Williams' cache—that, and the conviction that it was his only chance to best Dawley without killing him.

Williams' cache, he saw when he came within half a mile of it, was on a level near a river—the Carrizo—for he knew it. It doubled back sharply at a little distance west of the cache, swinging wide and running south into the Canadian.

Snug in the thrust of land near the river was a timber grove. In a wide clearing in the timber rose the roofs of a number of shanties. There were a score or more of them, facing one another over a vacant space which answered as a street, but which was merely a sand level, hard, dry, and dusty. When Burgess drew closer, however, he saw that the vacant space was in reality a three-sided court.

Hitching-rails fringed some of the buildings, with several horses standing near them, and as Burgess swung out of the saddle in front of a building near the center of the row on his right, he saw several men—and two or three women—watching him from doors and windows.

The interest in the eyes of the watchers, Burgess noted as he threw swift, furtive glances around him while tying Darkey, was not the casual curiosity with which the average cow town greets every new arrival, but a speculative and intent wonder not unmixed with frank hostility.

But Burgess was unperturbed; he had expected hostility in Williams' cache—and suspicion. After tying Darkey, he straightened and glanced about him. For the first time, he seemed to note the watchers, and he grinned mildly at several men who were standing just inside the door of a building in front of which he had tied his horse. Burgess' glance, after sweeping the men in the doorway, went to a sign just above the door—a crudely wrought affair which bore the legend: "Joe's Saloon."

Not hesitating, Burgess stepped toward the door. He noted a concerted stiffening of bodies as he reached the threshold, and stealthy movements of hands toward pistol butts. But he paid no attention to these signs of hostile expectation, continuing his progress toward the interior of the room.

There was a sullen movement as he stepped over the threshold; the men in the group near the door shifted slowly, permitting him to pass between them.

Inside, along the left wall, was a bar. Half a dozen men stood before it drinking. Burgess felt their eyes on him as he felt the gaze of half a dozen other men who were playing cards at a nearby table.

Behind the bar a huge bearded man looked inquiringly at Burgess as the latter faced him.

"Your best," said Burgess, meeting the man's intent gaze. He turned carelessly, and many glances that had been boring into his back were shifted to his face. For an instant he stood silent, looking from one to another of them with a frank, engaging smile.

"Surge up, gentlemen," he said then. "It's my treat."

For an instant there was a silence. Burgess wheeled slowly and filled a glass from a bottle that the barkeeper had set before him. For a little space, during which Burgess set the bottle down and looked speculatively at the glass he held in hand, the silence continued, and it seemed that his invitation was not to be accepted. Then a chair grated on the floor, a step sounded, and a man walked to the bar and stood beside Burgess.

Burgess turned to him, grinning.

"I reckoned that maybe I'd have to drink alone," he said.

"Hell," said the other. "The gang was sizin' you up, I reckon. Strangers don't usual brace in here an' blow the house without sendin' in visitin' cards."

Feet were scuffing and spurs jangling while Burgess and the other had been talking, and now the bar was fringed with men who, while busying themselves with glasses and bottles, betrayed their interest in Burgess by watching and craning their necks to overhear what was being said.

Burgess had glanced twice at the first man who had accepted his invitation. He was of medium height—the top of his head reaching Burgess' chin.

"I'm some short of cards, myself, this morning," said Burgess. "Didn't have time to go to the printer."

The other watched him steadily, and at last, noting the grimly humorous gleam in Burgess' eyes, he smiled, drawling:

"Sort of crowded, eh?"

"Some. Last I saw of town she was vanishing some rapid to the rear, and me urging her on, plenty."

"Sheriff?"

Burgess nodded.

"Dal Coleman and me had a falling out. I had to plug him."

The steady eyes of the other glowed; his lips set into straight lines. He looked at Burgess with increased interest.

"You're the guy that downed Coleman, eh? An' cleaned up Mogridge an' Dawley! The news of that little rumpus has reached us. Discussin' it—pro an' con—we've reached the conclusion that you done a damn good job—good an' necessary. Dal Coleman was an ornery rat who would have made trouble for us—if he'd had the nerve."

The speaker drained his glass.

"My name's Kuneen," he said slowly. His voice dropped still lower, so that the man next to Burgess could not hear it. "Figgerin' to throw in with us?"

A gleam in Burgess' eyes answered the question, and Kuneen straightened, speaking aloud:

"Denby ain't here now. He's gone—somewhere. If you want to see him, bad, why, you'll have to hang around till mornin', I reckon. Needn't worry you none; these boys is good company."

He swept a hand around the room and stepped outward, indicating Burgess with a jerk of the thumb.

"Boys," he said when he had got the attention of the men at the bar, "this here is a guy called Slow Burgess—the feller that slipped Dal Coleman the ace he'd ought to have had long ago. Slow ain't allowin' he's carin' to hang around Paro no longer since he's had the mixup with Dawley and Mogridge, an' I reckon he's got thoughts of talkin' serious with Denby. Denby's gone, so I'm bunkin' Slow tonight."

Ten minutes later, after Burgess had again called for drinks for the house, Kuneen led the way out of the saloon. Halfway down the row of shanties on the side where they were walking, Kuneen halted and, pointing between two buildings, showed Burgess a cabin of more than double the size of any of the others, well built, surrounded by trees that made an inviting shade.

"That's Denby's shack," he said. "Lives there with Belle Carson—his—his wife." He led Burgess into the last shanty of the row. It was scantily furnished, but was clean at least, and Burgess found nothing to complain of in his first quick glance of inspection.

"You'll bunk here tonight if you stay," said Kuneen. "You'll stay, if you want to, for Denby never turns a man out. If he don't like you—" Kuneen made an expressive gesture. "That's the end of it. No argument there, is there?"

Already it had become plain to Burgess that Kuneen had not brought him to his shack merely to show him his bunk, for there was in the man's manner a definite, though controlled eagerness that was unmistakable to Burgess. He was not surprised when Kuneen dragged a bench to the open doorway and sat upon it, motioning Burgess to do likewise.

"What's behind your comin' here, Burgess?"

Burgess returned his look. The wrinkles around his eyes deepened—as they always did when his thoughts were quizzical.

"Just feeling a little desperate, I reckon," he said.

"Bah!" exclaimed the other, and met Burgess' look with one of scornful incredulity.

"I've sized you up," said Kuneen, after a little. "You don't run to the plug-ugly style no more than I run to it. You ain't no damn' fool—nor I ain't. If Dawley was after you, you had plenty of time to get out of the country. Where was you?"

"Holed up—in the brush back in the hills—getting cured. Mogridge nailed me."

"Too thin," mocked Kuneen. "I saw Della Bowen draggin' you away from the waterhole the day Mogridge plugged you."

Burgess' face had not changed expression at this startling bit of news.

"Where were you when she was dragging me?" he asked.

"Back in the timber."

"And you didn't offer to help her? Don't tell me you'd stand and let a woman—"

"Shucks!" said the other. "Della Bowen has drawed the line right sharp for this here outfit. There ain't none of them that can be prodded nearer than a mile to the Bowen shack. I seen you twice, after that. Both times you was kind of weak an' tottery. Now you've got solid on your pins an' you come here, instead of hittin' the breeze to some place where Dawley can't get his hands on you. Come clean. It ain't no use to try to run no whizzer in on yours truly."

Burgess smiled saturninely.

"Dawley would be lonesome if I left the country now," he said.

Kuneen sat silent, carefully digesting the remark.

"Well, yes," he said finally, "I reckon you *would* be gettin' even with Dawley. I don't wish you no bad luck, but I'm hopin' I beat you to it!"

He sat clenching and unclenching his hands, his face flushed, except for around the lips where the flesh was white and the muscles tensed, his eyes glowing with passion.

"I had a little ranch over there—the Bar K. Five hundred head. Dawley busted me—wide open. Rustled my stock, burned my buildings, and when I kicked showed me a fake bill of sale sayin' my stock had been rustled from another man. My talk riled him. He sent Mogridge after me, figgerin' to try out the new jail. I let daylight through one of Mogridge's deputies, an' since then I've been dodgin' around here. Don't dare to go back to Paro. Same as you."

"Any more of Dawley's friends here?" asked Burgess.

"Plenty. There's two kinds here—them that's bad because it's in their systems, an' them that's bad because Dawley's clawed all the good out of them. There ain't no love lost between the two factions. There's bad blood, an' it's gettin' worse. Denby don't take no side. He's a bloodthirsty devil, an' likes a shootin' match. He'll egg 'em on, an' grin when the shootin' begins. The bad guys here are bad all over. They've drifted in from all over the country—gunfighters, rustlers, tinhorns. They're itchin' for a fight all the time, an' pinin' away to shadows if they don't get one. If they can't start anything with some unoffendin' guy, they'll pick on to each other."

The speaker glanced downward at Burgess' two guns, tied suggestively to the legs of his chaps to facilitate their rapid removal.

"One gun is an irritation to most of the guys that hang around here," he said, "but two is a standin' invitation to certain trouble. There ain't but one man packs two in this here camp—an' his name is Flash Denby. He sure can sling 'em, an' the gang knows it. If you ain't a lightnin' flash at gettin' 'em out, an' a he-wolf for workin' 'em, once they *are* out, you'd better chuck one an' be mighty careful how you wear the other!"

"Shucks," said Burgess gently. "I've packed them so long, and now you're telling me to desert one of them. I never bother trouble till it comes wooing me," he laughed. He stood up. "You got a place where I can put my horse, Kuneen? Well, I reckon I'll put him there, then," he added, when Kuneen mentioned a leanto behind the shack.

Burgess stepped out of the door, and, with Kuneen trailing him, walked toward the hitching-rail where he had left his horse, and around which a group of men was now standing, laughing and talking.

CHAPTER SEVEN

Again, as Burgess appeared on the street, he became aware of watchers in doors and windows. In the atmosphere of the cache a strange hush had come, a flat, dead silence full of grave import.

Even the crowd around the horses at the hitching-rail, having noticed Burgess' approach, had ceased talking and laughing. Some of the men had retreated from the hitching-rail, and were now standing with their backs against the rough board front of Joe's saloon. Others were still lingering near the horses, but all, even though some appeared not to be looking at Burgess, had their faces turned toward him.

All, except one, who, his thumbs stuck in his cartridge belt, the fingers of both hands brushing the butts of his gun with a lingering movement, as though he loved them, was facing Darkey and rocking slowly back and forth on his heels and toes.

The man was tall, lean, and sinewy, with a thin, wolfish face. Walking slowly toward the hitching-rail, Burgess saw the man. His eyes blazed with a sudden, wanton fire. As suddenly, the fire went out of them and was succeeded by a gleam of saturnine amusement, and he continued to go forward, apparently unaware of the presence of the man.

Several times during his voluntary exile Burgess had witnessed scenes of which, he had no doubt, this was to be a counterpart. Sometimes he had seen it happen to others; three or four times it had happened to him.

Always, in centers of human habitation beyond the region of the law, the stranger is considered the legitimate prey of certain types of men. Occasionally the affair turned out to be farcical, if not ludicrous. But more often such clashes resulted in tragedy. Yet, inevitably, the stranger entering the average cow town was subjected to indignities which were intended to give the established inhabitants an idea of his character. He was "sized up," in the idiomatic phraseology of the country; the standard by which he was judged being always a dissolute, quarrelsome resident, notoriously fast in drawing his weapons.

Williams' cache, a rendezvous for the lawless element of a dozen counties, the haven of men whose instincts and impulses moved them to violate and to resist authority, would size up a stranger also. Burgess had expected it, and had been mildly surprised that it had not been attempted while he had been inside the saloon.

Kuneen, as he trailed Burgess, whispered at his back, when for an instant he got Burgess between him and the crowd in front of the saloon:

"Look out! It's Tulerosa! He's layin' for you!"

"Thanks." Burgess' lips did not move. Smiling faintly, moving forward with an unconcerned swing, not seeming to see Tulerosa, but in reality noting his every movement out of the corners of his eyes, he walked to the hitching-rail and began to untie Darkey.

"That your cayuse, stranger?"

With one hand resting on the reins that were still knotted around the hitching-rail, the other hand hanging idly by his side, Burgess turned and looked at Tulerosa.

The latter was standing, his leg asprawl, his thumbs still hooked in his cartridge belt.

"Mine?" said Burgess. "You've said something."

"Had him long?" pursued Tulerosa.

"Long enough to know he's mine," answered Burgess.

He looked at Tulerosa steadily across the space that separated them. Tulerosa did not change expression or position. With a contemptuous shrug of his shoulders, Burgess turned his back to the man and began to untie the knot in Darkey's reins.

Then Tulerosa's voice came over his shoulder, cold and insulting:

"Well, he's too good a cayuse for a chromo like you to fork!"

Again Burgess turned, very slowly, so that Tulerosa would not be startled into drawing the gun that, Burgess knew, he was eager to draw upon the slightest pretext. He grinned at Tulerosa after he had faced entirely around—the slow, irritating grin of the man who knows that violence is coming, and advertises that he is prepared to meet it.

"You've lost your chance, Tulerosa," he jeered. "You ought to have pulled before I turned. You're a dead man, now, if you let a little finger tickle the butt of one of your guns! You're fast, eh? Fast—and a killer!"

Burgess' hands were both hanging at his sides now. His guns were swung so low on his hips that his wrists almost concealed their butts from Tulerosa's view.

Tulerosa had stiffened. Almost imperceptibly his body had sagged until it was in a crouch. He stood there, his legs still asprawl, his thumbs still hooked in the cartridge belt, his elbows crooked and straight out from his sides, his chin thrust forward.

Plainly, Tulerosa had not expected Burgess to take the attitude he had taken, and by doing the unexpected Burgess had his enemy at a disadvantage. There was a shadow of doubt in Tulerosa's eyes, though he was rigid, every muscle strained in expectancy.

Aware of the advantage he had created, and grimly appreciative of Tulerosa's temporary mental confusion, Burgess pressed slightly forward toward his adversary, a look in his eyes that caused Tulerosa to glance quickly and furtively sidewise, like an animal driven into a corner and seeking a way out.

Tulerosa was breathing fast. In the silence that had fallen the shrill heave of his lungs told of the tension he was laboring under; and each succeeding second his eyes grew wider as rage and resolution grew under the impetus of Burgess' cold contempt of him.

Tulerosa thought he saw Burgess' eyes waver ever so little. His muscles were rippling preparatory to a quick movement of the hands toward his guns, when Burgess' voice, cold and snapping, again threw him off his mental balance:

"Back up, Tulerosa! Back and draw! I'm going to shoot!"

Tulerosa gasped. The man was playing with him! The insane rage that seized him over that conviction glowed in his eyes, and the quick flip of his hands at his hips followed so rapidly that the watchers in front of the saloon did not see them move.

And yet the movement was tardy. Wrapped around the butts of the pistols, Tulerosa's hands had hardly stiffened for the quick pull, when streaks of blue-white smoke and fire spat viciously from Burgess' sides.

It seemed to Kuneen, standing near and a little to one side, that Burgess had fired once, merely, with each pistol, for he had seemed to hear only two reports. But he knew better. His eyes had told him what his ears had not—that Burgess had fired four times, twice with each weapon. The flame streaks had been nearly continuous, but Kuneen had noted an infinitesimal interval between them.

Tulerosa had staggered. He still stood, his legs still asprawl, but now his hands were hanging helplessly at his side; his pistols were still in their holsters. The man's face was seamed and drawn with pain, and there was pale, naked astonishment in his eyes as he glared at Burgess.

After a dull, flat second of stunned immobility and silence, a man darted forward out of the crowd to Tulerosa's side. He examined Tulerosa's hands and arms, one after the other, and then turned to his fellows who had not moved, crying in open-mouthed amazement:

"Four times! Both arms an' hands is salivated!"

"Hell!" exclaimed another man, as he ran to Tulerosa.

The incident was ended. Or had it merely begun? For, though the men pressed around Tulerosa, looking at his hands and arms, and variously commenting, and at last leading him into the saloon, giving to the affair an appearance of finality, there were looks cast at Burgess that were significant of future trouble.

"Lord, man!" said Kuneen, as with Burgess they went down the street, Burgess leading Darkey. "I never saw anything like it! But they say that Denby—"

Burgess grinned. "Did you notice my Darkey horse?" he said. "He never turned a hair. Must have a heap of confidence in me—you reckon?"

CHAPTER EIGHT

Kuneen advised Burgess to "stick around the shack" that night, for fear some of Tulerosa's friends, resenting the defeat of their man, might attempt reprisal. Burgess grinned at Kuneen over the little table at which they sat eating, when Kuneen offered the word of caution.

"My guns ain't a lot overworked, I reckon, Kuneen," he said. "And I'm some curious to see how this camp burns up its nights."

"You're a damned fool, but I'm for you!" declared Kuneen. And when, after supper, Burgess stepped into the street, Kuneen was with him.

They passed two stores, evidently closed for the day, for there were no lights in their windows; a barber-shop, from the ceiling of which a single hanging-lamp glared, with a man in a dirty shirt working at another man's face beneath it. Another man was standing, one foot on a chair before him, inspecting the cylinder of a six-shooter.

"Sort of wild-looking, ain't he?" observed Burgess gently, as he and Kuneen passed the building.

"That's the Gopher," Kuneen informed him. "Does Denby's dirty work."

Burgess stepped back for another look at the man, fixing his face in his memory. Then they went on.

Disgust grew in Burgess' face as the examination of the cache neared its conclusion. There were many private dwellings, belonging to no one in particular, Kuneen said. Their builders—some of them—still occupied them; other owners had left the cache, some of them voluntarily and others through violence. The title to the buildings, Kuneen asserted, was tacitly controlled by Denby, who exacted a nominal rental for them.

Besides the saloons and the two stores there were several brothels, with painted women to be seen within them, hilariously laughing and drinking with men.

"Williams' cache ain't no Sunday school," said Kuneen.

"Let's take a look at Denby's shack," suggested Burgess.

Kuneen led Burgess along the edge of the clearing to where a wide path curved between overhanging trees. Away from the lights of the cache the darkness was not so dense, and after Burgess and Kuneen had gone a little distance into the timber and had reached the edge of another clearing, not so large as that in which the cache stood, their eyes became accustomed to the semi-gloom, and the starlight made the outlines of objects quite distinct.

Denby's shack was in the center of the clearing.

Evidently there were three or four rooms in the building. A lamp burned near a window in the front room, and another flickered its rays out through an open door in the rear of the building.

Between the two lights the house was dark, but the shades in the windows of the intervening rooms were not drawn, and both Burgess and Kuneen saw the outlines of a woman's figure as she passed the windows, going from the rear light to the one in the front of the house.

Burgess had halted Kuneen at the edge of the clearing, and now with a word of warning he shoved Kuneen back until both stood screened by some nondescript brush.

"What's up? I hope you ain't one of them guys—"

"Shut up!" Burgess' command made Kuneen break off with his mouth open to continue.

"Who is the greatest beast in this camp? The one most likely to take advantage of an unprotected woman?" demanded Burgess.

"There's a heap of 'em." Kuneen looked hard at Burgess. "But I reckon Dude Dunham would be about the meanest, if you'd take him all around."

"Tall man?" questioned Burgess sharply. "White shirt, black hat, soft boots?"

"That's him. What you gettin' at?"

Burgess laughed.

"If Belle Carson ain't on the square with Denby we'll sneak back to your shack and turn in," he said. "If she *is* square we'll hang around here for a few minutes."

"Talk, you damned fool!" demanded Kuneen excitedly. "What you gettin' at? Spit it out."

"I wouldn't interfere in a clandestine love meeting," grinned Burgess—"that is, where the woman is willing. But if she ain't willing, and a man's trying to be a beast, why, then—"

"Oh, Lord!" groaned Kuneen. "Get it out of you!"

"Have you seen Belle Carson mooning at Dude Dunham— any time?" drawled Burgess.

"No—she ain't made no moon-eyes at Dunham. But she's busted him in the jaw two or three times for crowdin' her. An' more, she put Denby wise every time. The boys looked for Denby to kill Dunham. But he didn't. Just warned him. Heard Denby tell him myself that if there was another time it'd be the last."

"Well, I wanted to be sure," said Burgess. "And now I reckon we'll hang around some, for when you told me back there a piece that the cache wasn't any Sunday school, I saw a guy that might be Dude Dunham riding a big bay horse around the last shack. He was heading toward the timber, and he was acting mighty suspicious—like he didn't want anyone to see him."

"Shucks. Goin' to rustle some cattle, I reckon."

Burgess laughed shortly. "If you'd look pretty hard maybe you could see Dunham's bay horse standing in that brush over there—just where that little streak of light from the window is hitting him."

He pointed out the post and Kuneen exclaimed sharply, so that Burgess placed a hand quickly over his mouth.

"There's times when it pays to go slow," said Burgess, "and maybe this is one of the times. If a woman is wrong, why, that's her fault. But if she's right and the man is wrong, there's bound to be trouble. I reckon we won't interfere none until we're sure."

Evidently Belle Carson was "right"—at least, so far as her attitude toward the nocturnal visitor was concerned. For Burgess had hardly ceased speaking before there came a muffled scream from the house.

Burgess leaped forward, heading toward the open door at the rear of the house. He had to cross an open space, thickly dotted with chaparral growth, but he hurdled most of it, moving like a streak, and leaving Kuneen, who was not so agile, many feet behind. Indeed, Kuneen was not more than halfway to the house when he saw Burgess go through the open doorway.

By the time Kuneen reached the door another scream reached his ears; then a confusion of sound; then a short, pregnant silence. Then a shot, followed by a sharp, startled curse, which was instantly succeeded by a heavy, jarring noise such as would be made by a body falling.

When Kuneen reached the door that led to the room in the front of the house, where the light had been, he was confronted by an inky blackness that brought him to a halt. He heard a woman sobbing softly near him, and, seeming to come from a far corner of the room, he heard a man breathing heavily, shrilly, as though he fought for his breath; and there was a sound of threshing legs that smote Kuneen's senses as being of dire significance.

He searched frenziedly for a match, but it seemed that an age elapsed before he finally found one and lighted it. Then, as it flared up, he saw Belle Carson leaning against the wall near him, her hands pressing her breast, her hair disheveled, while on the floor in a far corner lay Dude Dunham, flat on his back, his legs threshing impotently about. Astride him, both hands buried in Dude's throat, the fingers exerting a pressure that was rapidly turning Dude's face black, was Burgess.

Burgess grinned over his shoulder as the flare of the match lighted the room.

"He kicked the lamp over," said Burgess. "Tried to bore me—him hiding behind the lady. I had to be real earnest with the cuss. Get the other light."

Kuneen dived for the kitchen and returned instantly with the other lamp. By the time he placed it on a small center table in the front room, Burgess had got up and was looking down at Dude Dunham, who was stretched out prone, unconscious.

"Get his rope, Kuneen," ordered Burgess.

And when Kuneen reappeared with a rope that he had taken from the pommel of the saddle on the bay horse, Burgess tied Dude's hands and feet. He got up, after the task was completed, and smiled at Belle Carson.

"Anything that's to be done further with him, ma'am, ought to be done by your husband. I reckon, if I was the husband, I'd want to talk to him a little. He didn't scare you a heap, did he, ma'am?"

The grin on Burgess' face did much toward restoring Belle's composure.

"I reckon you do feel pretty much unstrung, ma'am," he said, stepping close to her. "But you buck up and quit crying. I reckon

Dunham thinks you're some fighter, now. You scratched his ugly mug up considerable." His grin, as he stood close to her, was gentle and reassuring.

Kuneen, standing near, smiled cynically. He knew the Carson woman, and was not misled. And now, as Burgess grinned at her and Kuneen saw the covert, admiring glance she shot back at him from under the lowered lashes of her eyes, the cynical smile on Kuneen's face deepened.

Nor was Kuneen surprised when Belle, feeling Burgess' hand patting her arm with that comforting lightness, impersonal and earnest, which sympathy extends to distress, leaned suddenly forward and buried her head on his shoulder, saying softly:

"Don't leave me, please. And have Dunham taken away."

Kuneen's cynical smile became a mixture of cynicism and jeering joy as he caught the expression of Burgess' face. For Burgess, astonished over Belle's action, had stiffened to hold the weight that had suddenly been thrown against him. His hands were hanging limply at his sides—as though they had suddenly become encumbrances that had no functions to perform; and his face was red with an embarrassment so deep and sincere that the sight of it caused everything but the jeering joy to leave Kuneen's eyes.

"I reckon you're right, ma'am," said Kuneen, grinning hugely at Burgess. "I'll tote the Dude over to Joe's an' have Joe set a guard over him till Denby comes back. I don't blame you a heap for not wantin' to be alone—they's a lot of such sneaks as the Dude in this here camp. But Burgess, here, will take care of you, I reckon, ma'am. He's had a heap of experience in that line."

His huge grin became more huge as Burgess frowned at him. But he paid no more attention to the frown. Stooping, he swung the Dude over his shoulder and carried him out.

Burgess, the flush on his face gradually disappearing, the frown slowly changing to a reluctant appreciative grin, heard Kuneen's retreating footsteps. When they told him that Kuneen had crossed the threshold of the outside door, he raised his arms to Belle's shoulders and gently but firmly forced her backward until she stood facing him, an arm's length away.

"I reckon you're all right now, ma'am. I'm certainly glad that I've been able to be of some service to you. But the Dude's gone now, and Kuneen. And I reckon I'll be going, too."

"I'm sure I can't thank you enough." Miraculously, the tears had dried, and she was meeting his gaze with an engaging smile. "I really wasn't afraid of the Dude, I believe," she added. "He is a beast, and I despise him. But you came—just in time, I think. You are new to the camp, aren't you? I have never seen you before."

"I reckon not, ma'am. I got here this morning."

"And your name?"

"Burgess."

"Oh," she said lowly, and looked at him curiously, "you are the man who shot Tulerosa. Tulerosa is a most dangerous man. I have heard Denby say that Tulerosa is the most dangerous man in the country. Were you not afraid?"

"Of Tulerosa?" Burgess smiled. "You see, I didn't know Tulerosa, ma'am, never having met him."

"Then you are a stranger in the country?"

"I reckon I could say that. I've just got back, after being away from Paro since I was a kid."

"I remember now." A deepening interest was in her eyes. "Denby said something about you. You are called Slow Burgess, aren't you? And you returned to Paro to find Dave Dawley in possession of your father's property. You had a fight, and Dal Coleman was killed. Mogridge and Dawley and Judge Quinn say you killed him. Did you?"

He grinned.

"I wasn't such an awful distance away when the pistol that killed him went off."

"And you came here to escape Dawley." There was a flash of malice in her eyes. "Dawley has sent many a good man here."

"Thank you, ma'am." There was mockery in his eyes now.

"But you are a good man," she protested, noting his look. "Otherwise Tulerosa would now be gloating over you." She smiled at him. "Won't you sit down? It is terribly lonesome here. Denby is jealous—of course—and has forbidden any of the men to come here. But you are here, you know, and have done Denby a service, and you have my gratitude, and—and I rather think Denby wouldn't object. Anyway," and her smile grew significant, "Denby isn't here now."

"Kuneen will be wanting me, ma'am," he lied. "I've promised him a game of cards."

"Do I look dangerous?" She smiled at him and watched him until, swinging through the adjoining room, his spurs jangling musically on the carpeted floor, he reached the kitchen. Then he turned, answered her smile, and stepped down into the darkness of the clearing.

Kuneen fell in behind him, and they found the path leading to the cache. They had made their way halfway down the path before Kuneen spoke—and the latter's voice was a blurting whisper.

"I'd been watching you for a little while through the window—from the brush, here," said Kuneen. "That woman's a she-devil, an' no mistake! She took a shine to you, immediate, an' you're going to have your hands full if you hang around here any time at all. I was sure tickled when you didn't fall for her soft-soapin' an' smilin'. You'd have been a dead man by now, if you had!"

"Why?"

"Denby's here. He was in Joe's place when I toted the Dude in. When I told him what had happened he give orders to truss the Dude up an' leave him in Joe's back room till mornin'—when he'd tend to him. Then he lit out for his shack, an' I followed him, hidin' behind the brush with my gun bent on him. He was pikin' you an' Belle off through the front window. An' he'd have salivated you sure, if there'd been any moonin' between you two." Kuneen heaved a deep sigh of relief. "I reckon the Lord does take care of his fools—sometimes," he concluded.

Burgess laughed.

"The Lord—and a fool's eyes, in this case, Kuneen. For I saw Denby watching us through the window."

Kuneen gasped.

"You never saw Denby before. How in hell did you know—"

"Well, maybe I didn't exactly know, Kuneen. But you'll admit I'm a mighty good guesser."

"An' you'll be a damn' sight better one if you keep away from that woman's rope, Burgess. For she's out for you, I tell you. An' Denby or nobody else is goin' to head her off. There's goin' to be hell to pay in this here camp from now on, an' don't you forget it!"

"You're a mighty good guesser yourself, Kuneen," said Burgess. "I reckon there's going to be hell to pay, all right. You don't reckon I came here to fritter my time away loafing, do you?"

"Now that you speak of it, I don't expect you to do any loafin'," said Kuneen, mimicking the other's voice and accentuating its slow drawl. "Slow—eh? How in blazes does anybody keep track of you when you get to goin' for sure?"

Burgess' low chuckle, floating back to him, made him curse joyously.

CHAPTER NINE

Shortly after breakfast the following morning Burgess was told by Kuneen—who had gone out early—that Denby wanted to see him at the latter's shack.

When Burgess reached the clearing near the house he saw Denby seated on the little front porch of the house smoking a cigarette. He was seated in a rocking-chair, a book in hand, in which he was apparently deeply absorbed, for he did not seem to see Burgess until the latter halted at the edge of the porch.

Then he closed the book, placed his left hand on it, and with the right hand took the cigarette from his lips. He blew the smoke straight outward, then flicked the cigarette away, looking at Burgess meanwhile with a level and intent gaze.

There was a hint of a smile on his face now, after he had looked at Burgess for some seconds without speaking—Burgess returning his gaze steadily.

The smile broadened as he opened his mouth to speak:

"You're Burgess, I expect. Kuneen tell you I wanted to see you? Take a chair," he added at Burgess' nod. He indicated another rocker that stood near. He twisted in his own chair so that he faced Burgess. "You got here yesterday—in the morning. What's on your mind?"

"Dawley, principally."

Denby scowled.

"Dawley's a slick crook," he said finally. "What do you think? Is he a trifle better or worse than the man who goes and takes what he wants without scheming to do it?"

"I don't admire Dawley."

The other laughed.

"You evaded a direct answer. I'm to think one of two things—that you don't like the straightforward method, or that you don't like either. Which is it?"

"If a man can take anything from another man by force he is entitled to it—if the other man is fool enough to let him have it."

"Which he generally is—where there is no law to appeal to," smiled Denby. "And what about Dawley's method—to steal with the aid of the law?"

"That's why I'm here," said Burgess. "I didn't think well of his methods. I'm against that kind of law." Denby continued to smile meditatively.

"You're like a number of other men that Dawley has sent here, Burgess. You're an outlaw from necessity. Almost every man that Dawley has sent here—broken—cherishes hopes that one day he will be able to square things with Dawley. You do, of course."

"Certainly."

"Dawley has you pretty well corraled, I hear," continued Denby. "You made a mistake in not killing him when you had the chance—eh?"

Burgess laughed.

"I thought of it. Why I didn't shoot him is a mystery to me. Unless I thought shooting was too good for him."

"I've had the same feeling," said Denby, and for an instant his eyes gleamed maliciously. "There have been men that I wanted to kill by methods that would have made the tortures of the Spanish Inquisition gentle in comparison. I reckon that's the sort of passion you have for Dawley. I have it now. I shall give you an illustration of it after a while. To get back to you.

"You came here yesterday, and within an hour you had put Tulerosa temporarily out of business. I've seen him. Your marksmanship was perfection. Tulerosa has two wounds in each arm—in each wrist and in each forearm. What is more, the wounds are about the same distance apart, showing that the thing was not an accident. You are a dangerous man with a gun, Burgess. Is that how you came to get your reputation for being slow?"

Burgess met the other's grin with grave eyes.

"I reckon I was slow with Dawley," he said.

"And with Tulerosa," said Denby. "I got it out of Tulerosa. It's against the rules here, to run that gunplay in on a stranger—until he's been interrogated by me and his status determined. Tulerosa was anxious to earn the five hundred that Dawley promised him to put you out of business." He leaned back in his chair and chuckled over the leaping passion in Burgess' eyes.

"Well, the mistake was excusable," continued Denby. "That little horseplay always crops up when a stranger fans into a town. But take care! Tulerosa may still have thoughts of that five hundred! And keep your eyes peeled for some of the others. There are men here who would cut your throat for the price of a drink of Joe's whisky!"

"I've met that kind before," said Burgess.

"You're going to throw in with us?" suggested Denby, after a silence.

"Yes. But let's get it straight. I've come here to be close to Dawley. I don't like your game. I won't play it. But I won't throw anything in your way. I stay here and run my own trail. If the kind of law represented by Dawley interferes with the cache I'll sling a gun for you. If that don't meet up with your views I'll slope right now."

"I rather expected that from you," said Denby. "And it's a direct answer to a question I asked you previously. You don't like my methods and you don't like Dawley's. But you like his less than you like mine. Therefore you want to stay with me until you can square with Dawley.

"I don't have to have you here, but I'm going to take you up because, up to now, I haven't been able to pay Dawley what I owe him, and I have a hope that you will. Stay, by all means, and you can turn your back when something happens here that doesn't meet your high idea of morality."

There was a sneer in his voice, but no malice.

"You were around my house last night. Why?" he asked, with a sharp look at Burgess. "Curiosity, I suppose?" he suggested.

"Curiosity to see what Dude Dunham was up to," returned Burgess. He told Denby of seeing the Dude riding into the timber, how he and Kuneen had followed the Dude and related what had occurred later. Denby's eyes gleamed coldly during the recital.

"I wanted to thank you—for what you did," said Denby, when Burgess concluded. "But I'm glad you didn't kill the Dude. Would you, in my place, kill a man for looking with longing upon Belle Carson?"

There was a vibrant, passionate note in Denby's voice now, where before it had been smooth and even.

"No man has a right to say what he would do in another man's place under certain conditions," he said; "because no man knows how he would feel under those conditions. But I reckon he would feel pretty strongly."

"You're right," laughed Denby lightly. "You are not much of a lady's man, are you, Burgess?"

"Why do you say that?"

"Belle told me you were so embarrassed over her leaning momentarily upon you for support—after you had guzzled the Dude—that she had a hard time keeping you in the house while she thanked you."

Belle, then, had been suspicious that Denby had been outside, watching. Mentally, he commended her nimble wit. He wondered whether Belle had volunteered that information or whether a question by Denby had prompted it. It made little difference either way, for his conscience was clear—he had no designs on Belle Carson.

"I reckon I wouldn't be looking for another man's wife, if I was a lady's man," he grinned. "It's mighty dangerous."

"Yes," said Denby, with a quick glance at him, "it's mighty dangerous. The Dude will find it out presently." He laid his book down and got up. "It may as well be now," he said. "Let's go over to Joe's and take a look at the Dude."

Burgess followed him through the timber to the street of the cache. As they walked toward the saloon Denby was variously greeted—always respectfully—as "Cap" and "Boss," one servile subject even affixing the prefix "Mister" to the "Captain."

They found the Dude, disheveled and hollow-eyed, curled up on the floor in a corner of the room in the rear of the saloon. A cache man, a six-shooter in hand, was sitting on a soap box watching him.

A number of the cache men had followed Denby and Burgess into the room, but they stood at a distance when Denby walked over to the corner where the Dude lay and looked down at him.

"Well, Dude," said Denby coldly; "you had to meddle—eh? Do you remember what I told you?"

Dude did not speak, but turned a despairing gaze into Denby's eyes. What he saw there must have convinced him that Denby would not be merciful for this third offense. He motioned to several of the men, and the latter lifted Dude to his feet. Then, obeying Denby's directions, they removed the rope that bound the man. They all stood silent as the Dude, stiff and weak from the cramped position he had been in, twisted and stretched, groaning and wincing at each movement.

The Dude's face was now ghastly white. Yet he met Denby's smiling and malevolent eyes with some degree of defiance, and made no protest when Denby ordered him to walk out of the back door of the saloon.

Every resident of the cache was in the line that straggled after the Dude as, followed within arm's length by Denby, he walked down the path, through the timber, toward Denby's house. Denby and the Dude were slightly in advance of the others, and none could hear a word of the whispered conversation that was carried on between the two. Yet the Dude went steadily, seemingly having given up hope.

He passed the house, skirting the porch where Burgess had sat talking with Denby. He walked perhaps a hundred feet out from the front of the porch. Then he halted, facing Denby.

"Here?" he asked.

"Yes—that will do." Denby was smiling. The other men—Burgess and Kuneen included—were standing near, but neither Denby nor the Dude seemed to see them. Burgess noted, with a sort of grim wonder, that one of the curtains of the front window in the house was strangely agitated; but he did not see Belle's face.

"I'm going to give you a chance, Dude," said Denby. "After all, I suppose you can't help being a sneak and a cur. It's in your blood. I'm going to give you a gun. You're to take it and turn your back to me. After you have taken twenty steps you are to turn and fire. But make no mistake—I'll start shooting as soon as you!"

He laughed, and, drawing one of his pistols, held it out to the Dude, stock first.

The Dude's eyes lighted with a wild hope. He stiffened at first, shocked by the chance of life that was being held out to him; then he grew limp and his knees sagged from the quick reaction. His mouth opened, his eyes grew vacuous. Plainly, his senses were doubting the reality of the scene.

But the feel of the weapon in his hand convinced him. His face worked with a savage joy, and for an instant it seemed he meditated shooting Denby where he stood. But Denby apparently had no such thought. And if he had the thought, he certainly had no fear. For he smiled felinely, standing in a careless attitude, looking at the Dude.

"Well?" said Denby.

Denby's voice made the Dude's muscles leap. He wheeled, walked rapidly about twenty paces distant, and, wheeling again, began to pull the trigger of his pistol.

Denby, it seemed to Burgess, was fatally slow. For he did not make a movement toward the pistol at his right hip until the Dude wheeled and began to shoot. Burgess heard men around him draw their breath sharply as they realized Denby's dereliction.

Did Denby count on the Dude's nervousness? Upon the effect of his cramped position on his muscles? It seemed to Burgess that Denby did, and that he was tantalizing the Dude with his slowness in getting his gun out.

For the Dude shot wildly. Every man in the crowd knew that. The reports of his pistol followed one another so rapidly that they seemed continuous. Smiling, Denby did not draw his pistol until the Dude's last shot rang out. Then the Dude's face writhed with impotent rage and fury. It was plain to Burgess that the Dude blamed Denby for his unsteadiness and his inaccuracy.

"You damned, sneaking devil!" he shrilled. "You imp of hell! You—you—you—"

He dropped the pistol and lunged wildly toward Denby, blaspheming.

His rush carried him only a few feet. Denby's pistol moved at his hip. He did not draw it out of its holster. At the flame-streak the Dude halted, staggering, clapping one hand to his chest. Swaying an instant, he seemed to recover, and came on again. Again Denby's pistol crashed, and the Dude's legs crumpled. He sagged forward, lurching slowly downward until he was stretched in a huddled, motionless heap in the grass within half a dozen paces of Denby.

Denby's smile was still smooth.

"Take him away, some of you," he ordered. And he stood off a little, watching as they carried the Dude's body into the timber. Then he walked to where the fallen pistol lay, took it up, looked at it, and examined it, loaded it, and returned it to its holster.

Burgess had not followed the other men. After Denby had restored the pistol to its holster he turned to Burgess.

"Well," he said, "I suppose the Dude suffered more during the few seconds when he saw his chance of life slipping away from him than I ever did over the damned jealousy he aroused in me. You saw his face, didn't you, when he found he hadn't hit me?"

Burgess nodded.

"And what do you suppose were his thoughts?"

"He was furious because he had missed you, of course."

"Wrong," laughed Denby. "He was furious because I had tricked him. He knew—but it was too late."

"Knew what?"

"That I had filled his pistol with blank cartridges. Bah!" he added. "Do you think I would give *him* a chance?"

CHAPTER TEN

For a few days following the shooting of the Dude, Denby paid little attention to Burgess. Denby's time, it seemed, was fully occupied between Belle Carson and some mysterious activity that kept him away much of nights.

Usually the cache did not see him after these nocturnal excursions until the afternoon of the next day. And then he seemed to spend much of his remaining time talking with several members of the band who seemed to be immediately beneath him in authority.

Burgess was little disappointed over Denby's habit of ignoring him. He had done nothing himself, except to wander quietly around the cache taking note of its buildings and learning something of the character of the men. Several times he had ridden over the level surrounding the cache, but he said nothing to Kuneen about these trips, though he was usually gravely thoughtful on returning to the cache.

He rode one day to Dry Bottom, a town seventy miles eastward, and spent another day watching the railroad builders stretching the rails westward toward Dry Bottom. He spent another half day making the acquaintance of the engineer in charge of the work, but could get no information from him.

"This road is sure going west," the engineer said. "But just *how* it's going west is a question for the eastern office to decide. I suppose it *has* been decided," he grinned; "but they haven't let me into the secret. If they'd put me wise I'd probably speculate in land sites and rights of way."

Burgess was not misled. His talk with the engineer had taken place in a little corrugated iron shack which answered as an office, and while Burgess had been talking he had cast several swift glances at a map which hung on the wall near him.

Perhaps the engineer did not know exactly the route that his road was to take after leaving Dry Bottom, but he knew how to read the map, and the hieroglyphics that appeared were no deep mysteries to him.

One route had been deeply studied, too, for dirty fingers, running it, halting here and there, had soiled it so that it was not legible at a glance.

But Burgess had taken several glances, and he had noted Paro City and Williams' cache. They, evidently, were not considered important, for the soil line was thin over the names, but the knowledge that they were there was important enough to Burgess to make his lips shut tightly with decision.

He rode northwestward to Fillets—over a rough, broken trail, crisscrossed with mountain ranges, hills, canyons, and other natural barriers that would make railroad building difficult. He spent two days making the trip, and another day northwestward from Fillets, and when he rode back into the town he was convinced that none but a company headed by insane men would consider building a railroad over the Fillets route when they might select a comparatively level country such as ran through Williams' cache and Paro City.

In Fillets he made some veiled inquiries concerning cattlemen in the vicinity of Williams' cache. And after securing the information he wanted he rode southeastward, passing the cache at a distance of several miles and halting just at dusk at a ranch on the Carrizo River.

"I'm a drifter, looking for a place to light," he told the rancher, after he had accepted the latter's hospitality; and the rancher—who had told Burgess he was Bill Carey, and his ranch the Three Bar—and the latter's two sons—big, lanky, sun-browned fellows—had seated themselves on the porch for a smoke.

"I've got mighty tired of wandering around," Burgess went on. "And if I could run into a little stretch of good grassland—say, a half-section or a quarter—I'd settle down so quick it would make me dizzy."

"They ain't nothin' in driftin'," said Carey. "A man gits worthlesser an' worthlesser all the time, until fin'lly he ain't no good for nothin'."

One of the sons turned to his father and chuckled slowly.

"Yuh might sell him that parcel of hell you own around Williams' cache, pap," he suggested.

The older man guffawed.

"So I might—if he was damn fool enough to buy it! It's dawg-gone raw now, ain't it, stranger? Burgess you say your name is? Any relation to Bill Burgess, that died last year over in Paro?"

"His son."

"Well, now!" Carey smoked thoughtfully, while his sons remained silent, watching him. "An' you're lookin' to buy land. Seems to me your dad had a heap of it when he shuffled off. Don't you come in for none of it?"

Burgess laughed shortly.

"Dave Dawley's got it—everything," he said.

"Cheated you out of it, I reckon," said the rancher. "If you was to go into details I reckon you couldn't tell me any more about it than I can guess. Dawley's a damn' crook, an' that judge he's got over there is a jumpin' jack outa hell. They've hornswoggled you—eh?

"Well, as I was sayin', it's dawggone raw now, ain't it? I've got a half-section of land over near the cache. I reckon the cache is about in the middle of it. I bought it from a settler named Cartwright eight or nine years ago. It was gov'ment land, an' Cartwright had proved up on it, an' I reckon you'll find my title right an' clear in the records that that ol' devil Judge Quinn is settin' on over in Paro.

"There's about two hundred thousand acres of land around there that ain't got no gov'ment to run it. They've legislated it around, pro an' con, playin' legal bean-bag with it until they've got it so balled up that they reckon it don't belong to no gov'ment—that is, it ain't a part of no state nor territory, an' they're just waitin' until someone comes along to tell them where they're at—which ain't at all likely.

"I ain't got no hope of ever doin' anything with that half-section, for it's too close to the cache, an' a man might just as well give Flash Denby his cattle right away as to try an' range them on that half-section.

"Flash Denby's as safe as if he was down in the middle of Africa. They ain't no law botherin' Denby, an' it ain't likely any law will bother him." He laughed. "I reckon you ain't lookin' to buy that kind of land?"

"Yes," said Burgess. "I'll buy it if the price is right."

The rancher opened his mouth to speak, then closed it, his teeth clicking sharply on the stem of his pipe.

"I reckon you got some object in wantin' to buy that land—besides wantin' to settle down on it?" he suggested.

"Yes," returned Burgess. "I have an object. I have an idea that in buying it I can make things interesting for Dawley. You've got three hundred and twenty acres over there. How much do you want for it?"

"I could git ten dollars an acre if the cache wasn't there. But, hell! It isn't worth a red cent as it is—an' won't be. If you mean business, I'd sell it to you for a dollar an acre, an' be damn glad to get rid of it."

"I don't want to take advantage of you," said Burgess. "I want you to sell with your eyes open—if you *do* sell. The new railroad is going through the cache—or mighty close to it. That's my opinion. Some day the land will be worth a hundred times more than you offer it for."

The rancher laughed derisively.

"Railroad!" he jeered. "Yes—I've heard somethin' about the new railroad. But the railroad an' the cache ain't goin' to jine. The railroad will skip the cache like a hoss shies at a prairie dog hole. Besides, if the railroad *is* cormin' in this direction, I got consid'able more land that it'll have to go through, an' them measly three hundred an' twenty acres ain't a flea bite. You've bought somethin' to worry about, Burgess, if you've got the nerve to take it!"

Burgess had the "nerve." The following afternoon he rode into the cache with a land contract in his possession.

When he slid off Darkey in front of Kuneen's shack the latter came to the door to greet him.

"Thought you'd got lost," said Kuneen, grinning. "Next time you go to gallivanting around the country you want to put a guy wise a few, so's he won't be frettin' about you."

Burgess' grin was as cordial as Kuneen's.

"Denby's gone again," he volunteered while Burgess was busy with Darkey. "Him an' most of the plug-uglies he ties to sloped the day before yesterday. Drivin' a bunch of rustled stock over the border, most likely.

"Most of them that's left in the cache is fellows that'd sooner not be here—if it wasn't for reasons that they ain't sayin' nothin' about. Joe an' Tulerosa is about the only ones of Denby's cutthroats that's left here."

In Kuneen's shack, when he and Burgess entered, were two men—a short, heavily built man of middle age, "Blacky" Pitt; and a taller man, younger, smooth-faced, glum-looking.

After Burgess had talked with the men for a few minutes it became apparent to him that both longed for the world outside the cache; for that freedom which they had been deprived of through Dawley's machinations.

Each had a different story to tell regarding the method by which he had been outlawed, and in both the yearning for revenge was strong and clamorous.

"We bin twistin' an' squirmin' in the cache like sidewinders with their heads shot off—doin' a lot of movin' around an' kickin' up a lot of dust without gittin' anywheres. We got the grit; an' every damn' man is itchin' to git at Dawley.

"But nobody knows how in hell to do it! That's what's botherin' us. Dawley's got us faded, an' we don't dare to make a peep. He's got a lot of deputies hangin' around in Paro. He's expectin' us to bust in on him one of these days, an' he's set for us. He's got the law back of him, an' we can't buck it strong enough to do any good.

"What we want is somebody with brains enough to cook up a deal that'll sorta git him to runnin' around in circles—like we bin doin'. Since you come here, me an' Blacky, an' some more of the boys which seen you throw down on Tulerosa, has bin kind of wonderin' if you ain't the guy to hand it to Dawley."

The speaker was the younger of the two visitors. Concluding, he looked hopefully at Burgess.

Burgess grinned at Kuneen accusingly.

"You been telling these boys here that I didn't come to the cache to loaf?"

"I reckon they seen that right on the jump, Burgess. You've had somethin' framed up in your head ever since you've been here. It's likely you thought it out *before* you come. You can trust these boys an' me, I reckon."

"Just how far will you boys go with me in anything I feel called upon to start?" asked Burgess.

Kuneen gulped. "The limit," he said.

The other outlaws nodded vehemently.

Burgess smiled faintly. "You boys have played poker, I reckon?"

"Plenty," came the chorus.

"Then you know that when a man's got a good hand he's acting like he hasn't, but he ain't letting anybody see his hand. Bucking Dawley is like playing poker—you just can't let him know what kind of a hand you've got. I'm playing mine close for the big showdown. Maybe I've got a good hand, and maybe I'm bluffing. The showdown will tell that.

"But if you're wanting me to bust Dawley you've got to play my game. No talk, and be ready when I want you. That go?"

The men nodded.

"All right," said Burgess; "I'll tell Kuneen when I want you. Don't let Denby or any of the others see you talking to me."

Later that night in the shack Kuneen looked at Burgess across the room.

"Belle Carson's asked me about you—three times," said Kuneen. "You've sure stampeded her."

Burgess did not answer.

"Tulerosa's gone," said Kuneen, after a while. "Went to Paro. It's likely Dawley will bust him wide open."

"What for?"

"Why, for not salivating you, of course!"

"How did you know?"

"That Tulerosa come here to clean up on you? Shucks! That ain't no secret at all. They was eight or ten guys in Joe's the night

Denby made Tulerosa spit it out, an' they all reckoned as how you'd someway wised up to what Tulerosa's game was."

"Denby reckoned that, too?"

"Denby? Denby didn't do nothin' but look at Tulerosa's arms an' wrists. He kept sayin' to hisself, 'H-m, h-m!' I reckon he was sort of paralyzed over that kind of shootin'."

Burgess chuckled.

"You don't say?" he observed, drawling. "Didn't he want to know who did the shooting?"

Kuneen grunted an affirmative.

"You don't reckon that Denby was just a little nervous, do you?"

"Well, some. An' he got sort of white around the gills." There was a silence. Kuneen broke it with a short laugh. "By thunder," he said, "I been wonderin' all along what made you plug that geezer so nice an' neat—an' pretty!" He snickered. "An' so you done it for Denby's benefit! You're figurin'—"

"Slow, eh?" mocked Burgess. "There's times when a man's brain just naturally won't work at all."

"Meanin'?" yelped the now delighted Kuneen.

There was no reply from Burgess.

Shortly before dawn the following morning, Kuneen raised himself on an elbow and looked across the room toward Burgess' bunk and found it empty. Kuneen got up, dressed, and went out to the leanto. Darkey was not there. Kuneen grinned and went into the shack to get breakfast.

By the time Kuneen was looking into the leanto Burgess was several miles from the cache. The sun was just showing a red rim over the ragged horizon when Darkey came to a halt before a cabin door and Burgess slipped out of the saddle.

A young woman, standing in the open doorway of the cabin, emitted a cry of welcome and delight, strangely mingled, at sight of Burgess, and an instant later she was standing just inside the door, her two hands held prisoners in the sinewy brown ones that had grasped hers.

"Where's Ben Davis?" questioned Burgess.

"He is down looking after the stock."

Ben Davis stayed long, and yet the time was short to Burgess and Miss Bowen. They went outside and stood for a while in the shade of the juniper-tree that had sheltered Burgess during many of the long, hot days of his convalescence.

Several times since Della had greeted him at the door he had seen a brooding, anxious look in her eyes. It vanished when she saw that he was watching her, but instantly he pretended to look away the brooding expression came again. Twice he asked her if anything had happened, and both times she laughed and told him that everything was as it had been when he had left to go to the cache.

Yet something had gone wrong. He was sure of it, and several times he launched oblique questions which failed to solve the mystery.

"Something's happened," he said finally, taking her by the shoulders and forcing her to look up into his eyes. "I've been trying to get it out of you by hinting, but you won't notice any hints. But I've got to know. I'm going to ask you straight, and I know you won't lie to me. What is wrong?"

"Dawley has been here," Della said slowly.

The hands on her shoulders tightened. She saw his lips set, felt his muscles contract rigidly. All the gentleness had gone out of him. It was the first time the girl had seen him in this mood, and she was fascinated. He was showing her a side of his character that contrasted sharply with the unvarying gentleness that she knew, and she drew a deep breath.

"What did he want here?" Burgess tried to speak gently, but there was a cold menace in his voice that was unmistakable.

"He served a notice of foreclosure on me. The amount your father loaned my father was three thousand dollars. To that must be added the interest—making in all about thirty-three hundred. Dawley says I must have that amount for him by tomorrow afternoon or the sheriff will sell the place."

"Dawley works fast, eh?" he said. "If there's any copper around anywhere, he wants it. Was anyone with him?"

"Mogridge."

"Mogridge say anything?"

"Nothing. Ben Davis was out on the range. Dawley asked me who lived here with me. I knew the circumstances under which Davis had left Paro, and I told Dawley I lived here alone. I could tell he didn't believe me by the way he looked at me; and when, before he and Mogridge left, Davis came riding up, Dawley looked at me with a smile and said: 'I thought so.'

"Davis had come close by that time, and he asked Dawley what he meant. Dawley told him that he had suspected all along that Davis was staying there, for Davis and my father had been very good friends. Dawley told Davis that he, Davis, might raise the money for me, or, failing in that, I could come over to Paro and dance in his dance hall for him!"

The girl's face crimsoned. Burgess patted her shoulder.

"I reckon there'll be a lot of folks dancing before long," he said. "He didn't say anything else?"

"That is all."

"It was plenty." Burgess was grinning now, and the girl felt that, after all, her trouble was not so great—for there was a confidence and resolution in Burgess' manner that somehow reassured and cheered her.

They went into the house again, and Della prepared breakfast for Burgess. While eating, Burgess related, at Della's request, something of his experience during his stay at the cache.

"You'll be careful of Tulerosa, won't you?" she pleaded.

"Yes," he said. "But not careful about where I bore him—if there's a next time," he grinned.

He had just finished breakfast when he heard Davis ride in.

A little later, while Della busied herself inside the cabin, Burgess talked with Davis near the corral fence.

"I didn't like the look in that sneak's eyes when he was lookin' at Della," Davis told Burgess, speaking of Dawley. "I wouldn't put anything past him. My fingers was itchin' when he told her she could come over an' dance for him, but that skunk Mogridge was a-fingerin' his gun mighty significant, an' they wasn't no chance to do what I'd liked to have done. But I reckon they ain't no way out of it—Della will have to let him take the land an' the copper."

Davis' face worked savagely. "I run into Dobble this mornin'," he continued. "He was on his way over here. Wanted to tell me about Jay Hammond. Your dad lent Hammond twenty thousand dollars to develop his land with. Dawley tried to force a sale on Hammond's land, an' he manhandled Hammond when Hammond went in to kick about it. Looked like he had Hammond licked, an' Hammond sneaked out of town.

"But he come back again last night, just before the bank closed, ridin' his hoss. Knowin' Hammond an' Dawley liked each other like a rattler likes a road-runner, they was a consid'able gang surgin' along when Hammond clatters into the bank.

"Dawley was behind the counter palaverin' with that Glenmere fello'. He didn't turn a hair when Hammond busts in, cold an' contemptshus, an' clutters up the counter with what he dumped out of his saddlebags. They was enough banknotes tumbled out of them saddlebags to buy all the patty de foi grass an' créme de menthe in Frisco!

" 'There's your damned twenty thousand dollars, with interest to date, you damned, sneakin' crook!' Hammond tells Dawley, lookin' at him over the end of his gun. Dawley sorta paled like, but he wasn't noticeable scared, so far's any of the boys could see. An' Hammond pursues: 'Count her, an' gimme that note you hold agin me or I'll turn this joint into a shambles, pronto!'

"Evidently Dawley knows what a shambles is, for he reaches in a drawer and pulls out the note that Hammond asts for.

" 'Certainly,' he says, ca'm like. 'That's all we wanted, Mr. Hammond, the amount due on the note. There are no hard feelin's, I hope.'

" 'Not no more,' says Hammond. 'My feelin's toward you is consid'able beyond that. An' I want to warn you that if I ever ketch you nosin' around my place I'll bust up an' scatter you all over the country!' With that remark Hammond struts out.

"What made Dobble sore," continued Davis, "was to see Dawley handlin' the coin that you ought to be handlin'."

"Yes," said Burgess, "my money. Where did Hammond raise his?"

"At a bank in Las Vegas, Dobble says." Davis turned a troubled look on Burgess. "I reckon they ain't no way for you to git that coin for Della, is they?"

"Just one way," returned Burgess.

"An' you'll git it?" suggested Davis, his eyes brightening.

"Yes."

"Then," said Davis, grinning delightedly, "I'll take back what I said about you before you run away to the cache."

CHAPTER ELEVEN

Dawley was in an ugly mood. He had passed the greater part of the day in the directors' room in the rear of the bank building, glowering out of the window over the plains in the direction of Hammond's ranch.

He had expected, on the day he had thrashed the man, that he had seen the last of Hammond, and today was the date set for the public sale of the Hammond ranch. It was a valuable property, and it had slipped through his fingers.

Dawley's thoughts were vicious ones. This was his third failure within the past few weeks. It had begun with Burgess.

Three failures? Four! At Spring dugout his men had failed to poison Burgess; his plan to either kill Burgess or take him prisoner had miscarried, resulting in the death of Coleman; Tulerosa had bungled his job at Williams' cache; and Hammond had managed, somewhere, some way, to raise the money to pay off his note.

Yet Dawley's bitter thoughts were sweetened with one memory. The face of Della Bowen persisted in coming before him. Once, when his thoughts dwelt on her, he smiled. She had treated him with scorn during his visit to the cabin, but he was convinced that before she would yield the title of her father's property she would listen with receptive ears to a proposition he intended to make to her.

Dawley's conception of the morality of women was influenced by his experience with the type that he had been compelled to associate with. He had noted—not without a certain rage—that he seemed to make no impression upon women who were worthwhile—which, of course, made them seem more desirable in his eyes. Della Bowen, he had seen, was of the desirable type. And watching her during the time he had been at her cabin he had felt a surge of passion that had lasted until the present moment.

Dawley was slightly worried about the large sum of money in the safe. Hammond had made a public incident of its payment, and there were men in Paro who would not hesitate at robbery. At noon he opened the iron safe in the rear of the banking room, saw that the money was still there, carefully closed the safe and twirled the knob that controlled the lock, went out and sought Mogridge.

"Keep half a dozen of the boys hanging around the bank," he ordered, "day and night until I get some of that money out of there."

It was dusk when Dawley went out to supper. Crossing the street on his way to the hotel he noted that Mogridge had obeyed orders. Half a dozen men, whom he recognized as deputies secretly sworn in by the sheriff, were lounging around the bank building.

After supper Dawley went to the Dawley Dance Hall. Its pleasures seemed insipid, the men grotesque; the women irritated him. Yet it was near midnight when Dawley let himself in the front door of the bank building and made his way upstairs to his rooms.

He did not undress, but threw himself in a big chair, closed his eyes, and stretched out to think.

There was no way of getting at Burgess except by unlawful violence. He had discussed the subject of the cache with the governor some time before, and the governor had assured him that laws would not reach the cache, for authority to extradite convicted persons from the cache was as indefinite and vague as the ownership of the title to the disputed territory.

Unlawful violence he had already tried. Tulerosa's shattered arms and hands testified to its failure.

One problem that bothered Dawley quite as much as the question of how to rid himself of Burgess was: What had Burgess been doing during the seven weeks that had elapsed between the time of his disappearance from Paro and the day of his reappearance at Williams' cache?

Recovering from his wound? The wound, Dawley was certain, had been slight. But if he had been recovering from it, where had he passed his time? Dawley had sent riders out to search for him. No wounded man had appeared in Fillets, nor in any of the insignificant towns scattered over the face of the country within a radius of seventy miles. Nor had a wounded man appeared a any of the ranches in the vicinity.

Dawley wondered if his men had looked in at the Bowen cabin? He had not thought to ask about that, because he had heard that Della Bowen lived there alone, and he thought it doubtful that Burgess would head in that direction, anyway. Fillets would likely be in Burgess' mind if he had gone in that direction.

Dawley had lit the kerosene lamp on a center table when he had come in. He had turned the wick too high, and the smoke from the flame was befouling the chimney. He raised himself, intending to turn the wick down.

Halfway out of his chair he heard a smothered curse, seeming to come from the street. He stiffened, listening, and was certain he heard sounds of a scuffle in the dust of the street. He turned to rise from the chair, but sat motionless again, his body slowly becoming rigid, when a cold, warning voice came over his shoulder:

"Don't move, Dawley!"

The voice belonged to Burgess. Dawley knew better than to disregard the warning. He could feel Burgess behind him; could hear his deep, labored breathing; he knew that one of Burgess' guns was not far from his head.

Yet Dawley was not frightened. With heart full of malevolent hatred for the man who had helped to spoil his plans, he sat, steady, looking straight ahead of him, his face red and bloated with the poison of his thoughts.

From the street below he could detect the sounds of stealthy movement—smothered, muffled voices and swiftly moving feet in the deep dust.

Burgess had not come to Paro alone; there were several men with him. The sounds in the street convinced Dawley of that, and his lips grew thick with a heavy pout.

Burgess came around in front of Dawley, and with one swift glance at his face Dawley decided that a false movement or a biting word would quickly end his interest in any further schemes. For a threat of violence awful and deadly was in the eyes of Burgess.

"Get up!" commanded Burgess.

Dawley got to his feet. The action was accomplished easily—with grace. To Burgess' strained sensibilities it seemed there was contempt in the man's feelings toward him, and Burgess' eyes glowed with hate—with hate and the imminence of action.

"Damn you!" he breathed. "Why don't I kill you?"

"You can't murder a brave man cold-bloodedly, Burgess!" returned Dawley. There was the trace of an ironic smile twitching the corners of his mouth. "I'm not armed, either."

"I want to kill you!" said Burgess. "One day I shall kill you! I'll kill you now—tonight—if you make a single threatening move. I'm after some money that belongs to me, and I'm going to get it!"

"There's no money here, Burgess," Dawley lied smilingly. "None that belongs to you."

"You're a liar! Hammond paid you twenty thousand dollars yesterday. I want it; I mean to have it!"

"I'll choke the life out of you some day for that, Burgess," said Dawley.

Burgess grinned mirthlessly.

"I'll give you a chance to try, never fear. That's why I don't want to kill you, I reckon, unless you force me. Go downstairs and open the safe."

For an instant Dawley hesitated, meeting Burgess' eyes and looking deep into them. What he saw there convinced him; and with a nonchalant toss of the head he wheeled slowly and walked toward the door at the head of the stairs.

He did not pause or turn when he reached the door, but went through it and, followed by Burgess, descended to the banking room. He halted for an instant in front of the safe, looking again into Burgess' eyes. Then he knelt slowly, worked for a short time with the combination, and pulled the door of the safe open. Then he stepped back, motioning significantly with a hand.

"It's in there," he said.

Burgess laughed shortly.

"Get it!" he commanded. "No tricks go, Dawley."

Dawley grinned felinely and stooped in front of the safe, lifting out several bundles of currency. He laid them carefully on the floor beside him.

"Put it on the counter!" ordered Burgess.

Dawley did as he was bidden, but not without a malignant look at Burgess.

Burgess backed to the counter and stowed the packages of bills into the front of his shirt, keeping an alert eye on Dawley. When the money was safely on his person, Burgess laughed.

"That's all for the present, Dawley. One of these days I'll call on you again. Open the front door."

Dawley unlocked the door and threw it open. Again he looked at Burgess.

"Go out," said the latter.

Dawley stepped into the street. All the buildings of Paro, with the exception of the hotel across the street, were dark. And only a nightlight, flickering on the desk in the hotel office, indicated that someone was astir there.

Dawley had speculated much on what had occurred in the street during his experience upstairs. Mogridge's six deputies could not have been done away with without firing a shot. The thing was impossible. He had no doubt that Mogridge had failed him.

But when, urged by the sinister presence near him, he reached a corner of the building he saw several men standing and one lying in a heap close to the wall of the building. In the dim starlight he could recognize none of the faces, but he knew from Burgess' confident manner that the men were Burgess' friends.

Dawley laughed shortly. "It isn't my fault, men, that the reception committee was not here to greet you. I assure you I regret the oversight."

"You'll find five of them over in the hotel barroom," he told Dawley. "If you want any receiving done, do it yourself!" he derided.

"Thanks!" Dawley's gaze again sought Burgess. For an instant they looked at each other, their hatred naked and bitter in their eyes.

"There's six men here, Dawley, that are yearning to kill you for what you've done to them. I brought you out purposely to give them a look at you—and to test their powers of resistance. None of them have killed you—have they? They won't. You know why? It's because some day—when I've cleaned up Paro City—I'm going to do that job myself!"

Burgess laughed deep in his throat—a sound that made Dawley grit his teeth with impotent rage—and walked toward the rear of the building, the other men following him.

A little later, standing where the others had left him, Dawley heard the rapid drumming of hoofs on the hard sand of the plains.

White of face, Dawley listened until the sounds had died away, straining his ears to follow their direction. Then he crossed the street and burst into the front door of the hotel. An instant later—and for many minutes following—there arose sounds of a commotion that threatened to burst through the walls of the hotel building. There were thuds as of fists landing on flesh; crashes that told of broken furniture; the tinkle of breaking glass, shots, and the falling of bodies. Then ensued a heavy silence.

Following this, Dawley strode out of the front door and across the street, to disappear into the bank building, where, in his rooms, he washed some blood from his knuckles and examined a powder smudge on a sleeve of his shirt.

Later two men staggered out of the front door of the hotel. One nursed a broken arm; the other was tenderly caressing his face. Still later emerged two others carrying a third. And behind them crowded a number of other men scantily clad, who asked various questions, to which there came no answer.

To no one did Dawley drop a hint of what had happened at the bank. The unfortunate deputy, whose loyalty to duty had resulted in his complete effacement as a guard, never knew why he had been attacked. He reported the next morning to Mogridge, deeply puzzled.

"The other guys was across in the rum room of the hotel, lickerin' up—which I was so dry, too, that I'd have give a lot for a guzzle. I'm moseyin' up an' down in front of the bank when I hears a whiz comin' from behind me. I knowed someone was crowdin' me, but before I gits a chance to fan my gun I'm lookin' at more shootin' stars than I ever seen before in one bunch.

"I remembers feelin' pretty sore 'cause I couldn't git no action on whoever biffed me on the coco. An' the next thing I remembers I was eatin' dust in the shadow of the bank buildin'. Do you reckon Dawley handed it to me like he did to them other guys? Which I don't sabe, 'cause I was 'tendin' strictly to business."

Mogridge was no more able to explain that than he was able to explain why Dawley had punished the recreants in the hotel barroom. He advised that the matter be dropped.

But Dawley had no intention of dropping the matter of the twenty thousand dollars. The ease with which the robbery had been perpetrated—the off-hand, though undoubtedly earnest manner with which Burgess had dismissed him at the end of the incident—had added force to Dawley's passionate hatred of the man. The smiling confidence in Burgess' eyes when he had told Dawley that one day he would kill him had convinced Dawley that he really meant it.

Yet Dawley was confident also. Behind him was the mighty force of the law—made more mighty through the fact that he could force it to be applied for his especial benefit. Opposed to the law were the forces of the cache—outlaws who had no status under the law. The outlaws were impudent now—and powerful.

But there would come a day when their power would wane—and that day was not far distant. For with the coming of the new railroad—when once the iron rails were laid and locomotives were thundering over them, connecting those places where the law was most firmly enthroned—Dawley could more easily apply the force that he yearned to apply. But before the railroad could come—even though he had failed three times—he hoped to devise some scheme which would remove the man who had already troubled him more than any other man had ever troubled him before.

Early in the afternoon, accompanied by Mogridge, he rode to the Bowen cabin. He had told Della Bowen the day before the robbery that he would call this afternoon for the money, and when he and the sheriff halted their horses in front of the door of the cabin Dawley's thoughts were pleasant. He was certain that she had not succeeded in raising the money, and when he saw her standing in the doorway, looking at him, smiling and composed, though a little white around the lips, a doubt afflicted him.

"Well, Miss Bowen," he said gravely, "I am here again. I'm sorry to bother you, but business is business."

"Yes," said the girl, "you are very prompt. The Burgess estate must need the money very badly." She smiled calmly, and looked him straight in the eyes. "Have you the note with you, Mr. Dawley?"

Again a doubt assailed Dawley. "Understand, Miss Bowen, that I have no desire to hurry you. These matters come up in their regular routine, and one should not neglect them. However, if you don't happen to have the money handy we won't quarrel about it."

"Quarrel?" she smiled. "Oh, no—of course not. It isn't necessary. Nor will it be necessary for me to accept your invitation to dance for you. Though I never would have done that, of course. Will you please let me have the note, Mr. Dawley?"

"Certainly." He drew it out of a pocket and extended it to her, smiling, still unwilling to believe she had the money to redeem the note.

She studied the paper for a moment, saw that it was what it purported to be, then folded it carefully, tucked it into the bosom of her dress, turned and walked to a shelf on the opposite side of the room.

Dawley watched her, scowling. She returned instantly, still smiling, and placed a buckskin bag in Dawley's hands. The contents of the bag crackled as Dawley's fingers closed on it, and he looked sharply at her. The disappointment in his eyes was so apparent that the smile on her face grew—though he could see that her lips worked stiffly, as though some emotion, deep and breathless, had clutched her.

Dawley untied the rawhide thongs that secured the mouth of the bag and dumped the contents into a hand. A crumpled roll of bills fell out. Mechanically he counted them.

Several silver dollars added to the other money made exactly the sum, with interest, specified in the note. Dawley restored the money to the bag, dropped the bag into a pocket, and looked at Miss Bowen with a queer, intent, puzzled smile.

"One cannot refuse to believe his senses, Miss Bowen. I don't mind saying that you have surprised me—I didn't expect you could lay your hands on that much money at such short notice. You have done it, however, and—"

"And that seems to end our business relations," said Miss Bowen. "That is so, isn't it, Mr. Dawley?" And when she caught his short nod she went on coldly: "That is all, isn't it? I am very busy. There is nothing more to say, is there?"

Dawley took the dismissal with a smile.

"I think that is all, Miss Bowen."

He started to mount his horse, hesitated, looked at the girl, then wheeled again and climbed into the saddle. Riding close to the door he leaned far over and smiled at her.

"By the way, Miss Bowen," he said, "was Clay Burgess very badly hurt when he came here?"

She fought hard to keep the telltale flush from creeping into her face. The effort at repression made her muscles stiffen, so that Dawley's answer came without words. He grinned smoothly.

"I've been wondering who took such good care of him," he said mockingly. Sweeping his hat from his head with a derisive gesture, he urged his horse on, looking back after riding a little distance to see Della Bowen still standing in the doorway.

His back to the girl, Dawley scowled, and for half the distance back toward Paro City, Mogridge did not dare speak to him. Reaching town, Dawley went to the directors' room of the bank and dumped the contents of the buckskin bag on the desk in front of him.

His fear of robbery had led him to take some precautions with the money that Hammond had paid him, and as he examined the bills from the buckskin bag he discovered the secret mark he had put on a comer of each bill to make recognition easy. The bills Della Bowen had given him were some of those taken from the safe by Burgess the night before.

"Seven weeks," said Dawley mentally after a while. "They must have got pretty thick in that time." He laughed aloud, and the laugh had a measure of grim, pleasurable anticipation in it.

CHAPTER TWELVE

From the cache the next day Burgess rode to see Carey, of the Three Bar. Carey was glad to see him, and had some news for him.

"The new railroad is comin' straight from Dry Bottom, through the cache an' Paro City," said Carey. "My boys was over to Dry Bottom the day before yesterday, an' they seen some surveyors layin' out the line, an' drivin' stakes, an' puttin' up little stone monuments. They're comin' straight through.

"Just *how* they was comin' through without gittin' the consent of ranch owners bothered me a lot until yesterday I rode over an' had a talk with Mel Granville, who was consid'able of a lawyer in his time. Sometimes they *do* bother with gittin' options on rights-of-way an' that sort of thing, Granville says. But more often they git a grant from the gov'ment an' come through in spite of ranch owners, grabbin' the right-of-way as they come. Condemnation proceedin's, says Granville, an' injunctions, an' other writs from the courts they rarely use. Usually, though, there ain't no kick, because the country needs more railroads, an' the cattlemen are glad to see them come. But I've been wonderin' how they'll git through that orphan land around the cache—which no gov'ment ain't got a title to."

Burgess smiled.

"It's likely they'll crack that nut when they get it in their hands," he said. "Through Paro," he added meditatively, with seeming abstractedness. "That's off the line from Las Vegas.

A straight line now would take the road a good many miles north—say, about ten, at least, if I've studied the map right."

"So it would," agreed Carey. "I've studied the map myself."

"Besides," went on Burgess; "there's the new copper mines. Not one of them is nearer than ten miles to Paro. Hammond's place is the nearest, and that's fully ten miles from Paro. And there are two or three others—Bowen's, Munhall's, and Carter's—all cluttered up on what would be the straight line, if the railroad would take it. There don't seem to be any reason for the road going through Paro. And the north route is a heap more level." He smiled significantly at Carey. "Do you reckon that Dawley buying land around Paro has anything to do with the railroad going through there?"

Carey scowled and looked sharply at Burgess.

"By God! I hadn't thought of that! But I've heard it before. Mel Granville was sayin' somethin' about it. But I didn't pay much attention to him. I reckon he'd make a killing, eh?"

"Well, yes," smiled Burgess.

"The damned crook! That's why he's gobblin' everything over there!"

"I reckon," said Burgess.

"I bin wonderin' if they's any way to head Dawley off," he said. "Of course, you ain't interested," he grinned. "But if you was, now, an' you didn't like Dawley none, an' you was yearnin' to sort of disarrange his plans—like a fellow named Carey, of the Three Bar, is yearnin' to disarrange them—do you think it likely that you could suggest anything that would make him squirm?"

"You make me want to hug you," said Burgess, a leaping light in his eyes. "I've given some thought to it. If a man owned enough land—say a strip reaching from the hills back of you here—which no railroad builders would care to go through—to that stretch of broken country just the other side of the Bowen place—which a railroad couldn't go through—he might say certain things to a railroad company which they'd be bound to listen to. The strip I'm talking about being, of course, in No Man's Land—which there's been so much disagreement about."

Carey wet his lips. "Fifty thousand acres ain't such a hell of a big strip in a country like this," he said. "But I reckon it's big enough to make any railroad company set up an' take notice when it runs across the section you've been talkin' about!

"Look here, Burgess," he added gruffly. "You've been edgin' around here, probin' an' feelin' an' buyin' that little parcel of land over by the cache. Fightin' your own way! That's all right an' proper. You'd be a hell of a Burgess if you didn't have no fight in you. You don't recollect me, I reckon—'cause you was just a kid when you lit out of Paro, an' kids don't usually pay much attention to the old varmints that live around them. But there used to be a time when me an' your dad was pretty thick—an' he done a lot for me.

"There's some other oldtimers around here, too—Ben Davis, Dobble, an' some others. Some of them is lame an' halt an' blind, as the sayin' is, but they's times when they roam around the country. An' once in a while they run into one another. An' they will palaver."

He laughed at the expression of Burgess' face.

"You yearlin's think you are right clever—an' I reckon some of you are. But you've been schemin' an' plannin' around all by yourself, tryin' to figger out some way to whip Dawley. An' me an' Dobble an' Davis, an' some more, has been keepin' an eye on you. We bin figgerin', too. But they ain't enough ginger in the bunch to smart up the atmosphere none.

"You've got the ginger, an' you're a fighter. An' if them fifty thousand acres of mine is all that's keepin' you from herd-ridin' that damn' Dawley, you've got control of them from now on!

An' if you don't want any damn railroad to cross them, no railroad will cross! Now, get a-goin' an' quit beatin' around the bush."

Burgess got up swiftly. An instant later Carey was wincing and squirming and trying vainly to get his hand away from Burgess, who was gripping it vigorously.

"They ain't no call to squash a man's hand, Burgess; they ain't no call at all!" Carey protested. "That there hand ain't Dawley's neck—which I'm wishin' it was, though! I reckon if I thought you was goin' to get that excited I wouldn't have said nothin' about the land."

"Excited? Oh, no, Carey. Just tickled."

"Shucks—you're just' a kid, dawggone you; with a heap more muscle than brain, I reckon—or you'd have been over here before— talkin' straight an' not tryin' to ring-around-the-rosie with me! Git along now, yuh durn fool, an' quit makin' me wish I was thirty year younger, so's I could throw in with you!"

CHAPTER THIRTEEN

Burgess had determined to oust Flash Denby from the cache. That determination had been in his mind since the first day of his coming—and before. But, following his latest talk with Carey, the determination was strengthened. Denby and all his band must go. And they must go quickly, for it would not be many days now before the railroad surveyors would be trailing their stakes toward the cache—and the cache, Burgess had decided, must be ready to receive them.

Denby, Burgess had reflected, must now foresee the inevitable; that the coming of the railroad would make the cache untenable as a base for the operations of himself and his men. He wondered if Denby knew of the band of surveyors that had set out into the level west of Dry Bottom. If Denby knew, he hinted nothing of his knowledge to Burgess, and the second day following the latter's talk with Carey found him seated in Kuneen's shack, grimly impatient.

Denby had come in shortly after Burgess' arrival at the cache from Carey's, and it seemed to Burgess that Denby avoided him. Only once had Denby spoken to him, and Denby's manner had not lessened the disgust and contempt that Burgess felt for the man.

He purposely intercepted Denby the following afternoon as the latter was coming out of one of the saloons. Burgess had determined to question the outlaw in an endeavor to ascertain his attitude toward the coming of the railroad—if Denby knew of it.

"The new railroad is heading this way," said Burgess.

Denby halted.

"Yes; they've got surveyors out."

"That will make some difference, I reckon."

"Difference in what?" demanded Denby, with a sharp look at Burgess.

"In the cache. It won't be so safe here for a lot of folks."

Denby grinned mockingly. A certain stiffness of the lips as they twisted in the grin, a wanton and bitter malignance in the glitter of the outlaw's eyes, told Burgess that the man hated him heartily.

Why Denby hated him, Burgess thought he knew. When the outlaw had been standing outside the window, watching, the night Burgess had rescued Belle Carson from the Dude, Denby had divined what had been passing between Burgess and the woman. He had given Burgess a hint of his suspicions when they had been talking on the porch the morning following. And that suspicion, growing stronger as Denby had brooded over it, had become a conviction.

Burgess had seen the suspicion in the outlaw's eyes that morning, and having some convictions of his own regarding the man's character, Burgess was not surprised at the other's hatred.

But that hatred merely amused Burgess. His grin, answering the other's malignant look, was irritatingly knowing and provoking. Denby flushed under it.

"Not safe for you, eh?" he sneered. "Your yellow is showing, eh? Get out if you're afraid! I stay here; my men and me!"

Something in Burgess' eyes must have warned Denby; must have told him that another harsh word or another unspoken insult would have broken the tension; would have precipitated action swift and deadly.

Burgess, watching the man with something of the grim alertness with which he had watched Tulerosa, saw Denby's eyes waver almost imperceptibly; saw an ashen pallor stealing into his face.

The man was afraid of the clash that he had almost precipitated. Like others of his kind—men who killed other men in cold blood, as he had killed the Dude—Denby was a coward. His passions were allowed unlimited play when in the presence of men who feared him—when he held an advantage; but those passions were turned back, dulled, when he faced a man who did not fear him. They reacted, filling him with the dread that he wished to inspire in others.

Burgess had met men of Denby's type before, and he had correctly judged the subtle psychological effect the shooting of Tulerosa would have upon Denby. Denby knew that Burgess was clever with a gun. And now Burgess knew, because of the outlaw's naked fear, that Denby was convinced that he stood in the presence of a man who was more clever with his weapons than he.

Some men of the cache were walking toward the two, and in an instant more they would be listening. Burgess saw that Denby was aware of the coming of the men. A swift change came over Denby. He smiled, folded his arms over his chest, and spoke softly:

"Don't take offense at what I said, Burgess. I really am a little nervous about the railroad. But I'm going to stick it out."

He turned, and joined some of the men that had come up, while Burgess, disgusted at the other's exhibition of craven hypocrisy, went toward Kuneen's shack.

On the following morning Denby and some of the others were missing again. There was a rumor in the cache that they were after some cattle far down the Carrizo.

Denby's suddenly adopted apologetic attitude toward Burgess had prevented Burgess from saying to the outlaw what he had intended to say—that he had bought the land upon which the cache stood, and that the outlaw and his men must find another retreat.

Burgess decided to wait until the morning, but in the morning when he discovered that Denby had gone, one of those interpositions with which fate sometimes mocks man's plans did for Burgess what Burgess had puzzled over for two days—devised a plan that would bring about a clash with the outlaw without Burgess seeming to seek it.

That there must come a clash between them was now inevitable. For Denby had declared his determination not to quit the cache, and Burgess was equally determined that he should. And yet Burgess had hesitated to bring about the clash, for a clash between him and the outlaw could have but one ending—death for Burgess or Denby.

Burgess had just discovered that Denby had gone, and was striding impatiently along the edge of the timber near Denby's house, thinking of Della Bowen and trying to persuade himself that he ought to ride over to the cabin to see her, when, passing the path that led through the timber to Denby's house, he came upon Belle Carson.

She was standing in the shadow of some trees, near some thickly growing brush that screened her from view from the buildings of the cache, and Burgess was within two or three steps of her when he saw her.

There was a pleased smile on her face, and she made a mock grimace of disapproval at Burgess.

"I saw you when you turned the corner of Kelmer's store," she said. "And I waited for you. You have not kept your word about calling on me. Why?"

Burgess smiled, remembering the conversation between them that had followed the taking away of the Dude by Kuneen.

"I've been busy," he said.

"Playing cards with Kuneen? Oh, don't say that!" she laughed.

"Well," he smiled, "that excuse was as good as another. And I didn't want to tell you what was in my mind, for fear you'd get excited and spoil the scene."

Her eyes lightened.

"You saw him, then? I wondered, but I wasn't sure. I didn't see him. He told me—afterward—that he was there, watching us. I think he suspected, too, that we knew; that you, especially, had seen him. He hinted at it, with that delicate sarcasm that he so often employs."

She shivered.

"He frightens me sometimes—he's so sneaking, and creeping, and venomous! He's jealous, too, Burgess—jealous of you. I'm getting so that I'm glad when he goes away. But it's so lonesome here. Just look!" She turned, grasping one of his arms and facing him about also so that both were looking toward the house, and made a sweep with a hand that included the house and its surroundings.

"It's no place for a woman, is it, Burgess? It's appallingly dismal. When I first came here I rather liked it. The garden appealed to me, and the wildness—and everything. But I've grown to hate it. There's nothing to do. When Denby's gone I sit for hours, moping, looking out of the window, or sitting on the porch twirling my thumbs. Not a man in the cache *dares* to look at me, to say nothing of coming to the house. Denby has warned them. I am virtually a prisoner. It's giving me the horrors!"

Burgess asked her, rather gruffly, why she stayed here if she didn't like it?

"I've thought of running away. But I can't. Denby would kill me!"

"You want to go, then? But if you did, I reckon you'd—" He did not finish, realizing that he had no right to judge her. But she divined what he had been about to say.

"No!" she declared positively. "Oh, I suppose I look like that. But I couldn't—again. If I ever get away from here I shall go back east—to my mother."

Burgess' mild incredulity must have shown in his eyes, for he was thinking of her manner on the night he had rescued her from the Dude; how she had tried to lure him to stay.

As before, she saw the thought in his eyes. And again she reddened.

"Yes," she admitted; "I *did* want you to stay. I—I was desperate, with the loneliness, and the awful darkness of this place, and the thoughts that kept haunting me. And, before he left, Denby had beaten me—"

"Hell!" said Burgess.

"Oh, it was not the first time." She smiled, a hard look in her eyes. "He beat me again—after you left that night. That's why I haven't been out much since; that's how he got out of me everything we said to each other in the room that night! He knows, Burgess; he *thinks* he knows why you didn't let me persuade you to stay. He knows you saw him through the window, and he thinks you didn't stay with me because of that!"

Something had been added to Burgess' disgust for Denby. A reckless impulse seized him, conquered him. The inevitable clash with Denby was imminent. Why not hasten it? It was a satanic thought, but it reflected the mood in which Burgess found himself after listening to the woman's recital of the outlaw's brutality.

"Look here!" he said shortly, grasping her arms and wheeling her, so that she faced him. "Are you telling the truth?"

She met his gaze fairly.

"Yes," she said slowly. "Burgess," she added earnestly, "if I don't get away from here soon, I shall go mad."

He laughed, lowly and vibrantly, as he fought down the malicious impulse that had seized him. He had not lived a conventional life; the passions of the men and women he had known had been as his own, strong and gripping and ruthless, and those passions battled insistently for permission to return to Denby evil for evil. But he conquered them finally, and he laid a sympathetic hand on the Carson woman's shoulder, patting it as a big brother might have patted it.

She looked at him wonderingly. He laughed again mirthlessly.

"When do you expect Denby back?"

"Tonight," she said.

"Well," he said shortly, "tomorrow you can start back east."

He laughed again, and pushed her gently from him. Then he turned and walked toward Kuneen's cabin.

As he passed an open space between two trees he caught a movement at the side of one of the buildings. At a corner of the buildings he saw a man's face, wreathed in a malicious grin. It was the Gopher, the man Kuneen had called his attention to on the night they had passed the barber's shop.

Burgess had known the Gopher was watching them; yet he was glad now that he had conquered the impulse to pretend to make love to Belle. For the malice in the Gopher's eyes told him that the Gopher's evil mind would put a false construction upon the meeting between him and Denby's woman, and that when Denby heard the story of the meeting it would be lurid enough to sting the outlaw to insane rage.

CHAPTER FOURTEEN

About dusk Burgess had a long talk with Kuneen and his friends. In one way or another, without congregating in suspiciously large numbers, Burgess and Kuneen talked with every man of those Kuneen said could be depended upon to cast their lot with Burgess when a break should come.

There were twenty of these men; hardy-looking, eager-eyed, apparently believing fully in Burgess, and yearning for the downfall of the outlaw chief.

Burgess made it plain to them that the break with Denby was imminent, and he saw them stiffen and look at one another with eloquent, pleased glances. He left Kuneen with them, to unfold the details of the plan he had conceived, and shortly after dusk he sought out the Gopher; getting him, after a while, in a corner of the street.

"I saw you today, watching Belle Carson and me," said Burgess coldly, after he had crowded the Gopher into the corner and had one of his guns shoved deep into the Gopher's stomach. "You'll tell Denby; you're that kind of a man. I've no objections to that. But if you hint to him that Belle was to blame—so that he'll go and beat her again—I'll bore you so hard and fast that they'll be planting you before you know you're hit!"

He let the Gopher out of the corner and sent him down the street, watching him warily, for Kuneen had told him a few things about the Gopher's methods. And when he saw the Gopher disappear into Joe's saloon, Burgess silently sought Kuneen's shack.

It was a summons from Denby that appraised Burgess of the return of the outlaw. Kuneen and Burgess had just finished breakfast when a cache man brought word to Burgess. Denby, the man said, wanted to see Burgess on Denby's porch.

Though he knew what the summons meant, Kuneen paled.

"He's been stuffed plenty by the Gopher. You'll be mighty damned careful, won't you, Burgess?"

"You'll make me nervous, talking that way, Kuneen," grinned Burgess.

When Burgess stepped down from the door of Kuneen's shack he knew that the eyes of every man in the cache were upon him. A swift glance around told him that all of Denby's men had come in with him, and he knew there were at least thirty of them. They were watching him from doors and windows, and from the corners of buildings—for the Gopher had told them of what had happened between Belle Carson and Burgess during Denby's absence, and they were lounging around, awaiting the time when Denby would take his vengeance—as they knew he would.

They were wondering, though, how it would come. They had seen what he had done to the Dude, and though the end of that incident left them puzzled with the mystery of it, they were aware that Denby had somehow tricked the Dude. And they were wondering how he would trick Burgess.

Burgess, also, was wondering what Denby would attempt. That he would seek his vengeance without the assistance of others, Burgess was certain, for he knew the vindictive character of the outlaw, and felt that he would permit no one to participate in whatever vengeance he had planned.

Yet Burgess was undismayed. Those gripping passions that his antagonism against Dawley had aroused had held him in a mighty clutch during the past few days. They had hardened him and filled him with a lust to ruthlessly tear down whatever opposition reared itself between him and the goal he had sent out to reach—complete vindication and the ruin of Dawley.

Denby was standing in his way. That fact of itself would have been enough to drive out any thought of evading a meeting with the outlaw. What Belle Carson had told him had merely hardened him further.

He was smiling faintly when he reached the edge of the porch, for long before he came to it he had seen Denby seated there.

"Back again, eh?" said Burgess.

"Yes," said the outlaw. "Come up."

Burgess stepped, with apparent unconcern, to a point on the porch directly in front of Denby, resting his hands on his hips in a careless attitude and returning the look that Denby gave him.

Denby, Burgess saw, was fighting for his composure. The cordiality in the man's manner was surface emotion. Deep in his eyes was a wanton, cruel, bitter rage; the reflection of the insane jealousy that the Gopher's story had aroused.

Burgess gave no indication that he had noticed the strangeness of Denby's manner. He stood, waiting patiently for the outlaw to tell why he had sent for him. Denby tried to pretend friendliness as he looked up at Burgess. It so palpably masked the malevolent rage he felt that Burgess grinned felinely at him.

Denby sat quiet for an instant. But Burgess was not misled; he saw the man's muscles, trembling on the verge of action, contracting rigidly.

"There's something I want to show you, Burgess," said Denby. "I'll get it."

He rose from the chair. With a perfectly natural movement he placed his right hand on the arm of the chair, bearing his weight on it for an instant to aid his body in the upward motion. This brought the hand to a point just above the holster of the pistol at his right hip.

"I'll get it," he repeated as he rose half out of the chair. His voice was dry and light.

"This!" he breathed venomously, and drew his pistol.

The movement was as rapid as light. But equally rapid had been Burgess' movement. Denby's gun came out and fire streaked from its muzzle, the blue-white smoke curling upward as it passed between Burgess' left arm and side.

Only Burgess' quickness had saved him. His left arm had moved with Denby's right, and while Denby was pulling the trigger of his weapon Burgess' left hand was gripping Denby's pistol hand and holding it away from his body, so that the bullets passed harmlessly under his arm. But even before Denby's gun began to crash Burgess' own weapon was close to the outlaw's stomach, and its muffled reports told of the deadly execution it was doing.

The action, it seemed, had all been accomplished with one single movement. A breath before, Denby had been sitting in the chair, smiling his hypocritical smile at Burgess. Now Denby was on the floor of the porch, doubled queerly, but lax and motionless, with Burgess standing over him, a wreath of smoke curling lazily upward from the muzzle of his pistol.

Burgess leaned over and peered grimly into the face of the fallen outlaw. Denby would play no more tricks. Burgess straightened, threw a swift glance about him, and saw the men of the cache coming out of the timber at the side of the clearing.

The men were divided into two groups. Burgess saw that Denby's men were in the group that had formed on his left. They had, apparently, no suspicion of what Burgess and Kuneen had planned, for they were coming toward the porch, all curious-eyed, wondering, undoubtedly a trifle stunned over the defeat of their chief and the quickness with which it had been accomplished. Burgess waited for them.

Kuneen's men, he observed, were slightly behind the others, and slightly to their left—which brought them a little to the right of Burgess. All of Burgess' men carried rifles, while the Denby men had only their pistols.

As the Denby followers approached, Burgess stepped down from the porch. Both his pistols were now in his hands, and there was a cold menace in his attitude that brought the Denby men to a halt when they were within a dozen paces of him. Something in Burgess' eyes caused them to lose all their interest in the chief who lay motionless on the porch.

Denby's men, deprived of the leadership of a man they had admired and feared, and who had possessed the magnetism necessary to sway them as a unit to his rule, were suddenly smitten with indecision.

Had they been given time, they might have chosen a new leader, but in the stress of this moment they were undecided and vacillating. In the minds of most of them was an awed respect for the man who had played with Tulerosa, who had snuffed out Denby's life with such smooth ease and rapidity, and who faced them now, tense and alert—a dominant force that was undoubtedly hostile.

They heard Burgess' voice, cold and sharp, ordering:

"Hands up!"

They complied, mechanically, with black, wondering looks at the men who stood with Kuneen, armed with rifles.

A Denby man, with a swarthy face, who towered above the men around him and whose brain was working faster than that of the other men, grinned wickedly, first at Burgess and then at Kuneen and the others, and muttered raucously:

"Frame-up!"

There was a concerted stiffening of bodies at this word, and several men in the Denby crowd moved restlessly. The Gopher, partly hidden behind the shoulder of another man—with only his right side exposed, his face working malevolently—disobeyed Burgess' command and dropped a hand quickly toward his pistol.

With the weapon exploding and throwing up sand midway between himself and Burgess, the Gopher shrieked profanely and plunged forward and out, landing in a huddled heap in the sand near where he had been standing, while some smoke from the muzzle of the pistol in Burgess' left hand ballooned slowly upward and disintegrated fleecily in the air during the dead silence that followed.

Burgess' voice broke the silence sharply:

"Is there any. other man who wants to take Denby's end of this? Then listen," he went on, grimly aware of the statuesque rigidity of the others. "I'm running this camp from now on; me and Kuneen and his crowd.

"You men are through. Williams' cache is a thing of the past. I've got nothing against you except that you're like Denby, and Denby's kind don't go any more around here. I'm out for a cleanup. The cache is mine; I've bought it. The railroad is coming through here, and this place is going to be as pure and white as driven snow. You men can take your choice. You can hit the breeze out of the country, not stopping to argue, or you can start shooting now and take your chance!"

The swarthy-faced man laughed. He alone, of all the Denby men, seemed to sense the grim humor of the situation.

"Right clever, I'd call it," he said, while the men around him turned their heads to look at him. "I've seen, right from the jump, that you was goin' to be a burr under Denby's saddle. Denby wouldn't listen to my honeyed words of warnin'; an' as a consequence he's done passed out with his boots on. You stacked the cards on Denby, Slow; an' you've got 'em stacked on us guys.

"Law an' order, eh? Well, we ain't got no yearnin' for a camp that's goin' to be run on them principles; especial' when there's a guy doin' the runnin' which can swing his guns consid'able faster than guns has ever been swung in these parts before. I'm givin' you your own way, an' not clutterin' up the scenery promiskus if you're dead set on it."

Burgess grinned, his gaze roving from one to another of the faces that were again turned to his. He saw indecision depicted on some of the faces; upon others he saw dissent and malignant resentment. In the faces of others he noted incipient smiles. Many of the men were again turning to the swarthy-faced man, and it was evident that they were depending upon him to shape their decisions. He alone, of them all, had exhibited those qualities that hinted at the ability to lead.

Burgess' manner was abrupt and decisive. His glance rested momentarily upon the swarthy-faced man.

"I'm taking you up. You go, stepping right out to one side. One of Kuneen's men will get your horse. You'll go with him, taking what traps you want."

The swarthy-faced man stepped well away from the others, grinning. Apparently he was well satisfied.

"Hell," he said to some of the others as he followed one of Kuneen's men toward the cache, "it's time we was movin' along, anyway. Things is gettin' too crowded here. The railroad's sure comin', an' there's no use buckin' the things a railroad brings with it. Mebbe you guys has got ideas about stayin' here; but yours truly is cogitatin' a whole lot different, an' I'm slopin' while the slopin's good!"

He swung away after the Kuneen man, still grinning, and vanished behind the buildings of the cache.

Again there was a restless movement in the group of Denby men. Kuneen's men had slowly advanced until they now stood near Burgess, but a little to one side. They said nothing. Some of them were leaning upon the weapons, others holding them in their arms. But all their faces indicated quiet preparedness and changless resolution.

Had there been among the Denby men one reckless spirit with the personal magnetism to inspire to action the half-rebellious impulses that rioted in the hearts of the others, Burgess and the Kuneen men would not have won without cost the victory that now seemed imminent.

But no man with the naked courage to defy Burgess appeared in the group of Denby men. They stood, sullen—some of them scowling, glaring their hatred at Burgess; others curiously indifferent and passive; still others perplexedly looking at their fellows—until the swarthy-faced man returned, riding his horse.

"Still cogitatin', eh?" grinned the latter, eyeing the others from his elevation. "Well, she's a mighty hard problem to wiggle out of. I reckon from the way you're hesitatin' that there'll be some of you stayin' here, plenty. I'm hittin' the breeze to the border, not stoppin' to linger where there's goin' to be such a hell of a lot of law an' order! So long!"

He was away in a dust cloud, not looking back.

"Next!" said Burgess shortly.

The influence of example was too much for a man who stood near the outer edge of the group.

"Hell," he said with a reluctant, half-shamed grin; "I'm beatin' it, too. They ain't no damned sense of no man fightin' to stay where he ain't wanted!"

He stepped out. Another man, grunting approval, joined him. A third, crestfallen, ranged himself with the other two.

Their horses were brought, and, like the swarthy-faced man, they rode away. More men stepped from the group, thus signifying their willingness to yield to the inexorable rule of the man who so completely dominated them. When there were only a dozen left they were taken in a body to the cache and permitted to get their horses and other effects.

The situation that had threatened to become a tragedy had turned out to be a comedy, but a comedy which had placed Burgess in a position of vantage from which he could apply the lever of power which he hoped would dislodge Dawley, arrogant and ruthless in the fancied security of the law in Paro City.

Burgess, however, had not finished. The words of congratulation of Kuneen and his men were still in his ears when, with Kuneen, he visited several buildings of the cache and talked shortly and earnestly with their occuptants. The women—three of them—appeared after a time, anathematizing Burgess and his friends with strident-voiced invective.

Horses were brought, and the women rode away toward Paro City, followed by the derisive smiles of Kuneen's followers, and by Burgess' warning:

"Don't stay long at Paro!"

Alone, Burgess went to Denby's house. He found the Carson woman huddled in a chair in a corner of the kitchen, crying. She was dressed for traveling, however, which indicated that she was prepared to follow Burgess' advice about going east.

He got one of Denby's horses for her and helped her to mount. Then, telling her to wait, he got Blacky Pitt and sent him to Belle, telling Blacky to take her to Dry Bottom. Before delivering final instructions to Blacky, Burgess gave the man a number of yellow-backed bills and told him to hand them over to Belle when they reached Dry Bottom.

"They'll go a long way toward keeping Belle straight, if she's got any notions," he told Blacky.

That night Burgess rode over to the Bowen cabin. He had a long talk with Ben Davis. And for the first time he met Harvey

Dobble; who, before Burgess had left Paro City to begin his voluntary exile, had been a small rancher on the Carrizo River, within a day's ride of Paro.

Twice while Burgess was telling Davis and Dobble of what had occurred at the cache, the two men exchanged glances, and once, when Burgess made some reference to Carey of the Three Bar, Dobble's jaws closed tightly. Dobble, catching Davis' eye, deliberately winked at him.

"So you're goin' to do some buildin' at the cache," said Dobble, as Burgess stood beside Darkey, ready to mount. "Curious how things turn out, ain't it? Yesterday—or mebbe the day before—I was talkin' to Jay Hammond. Hammond's been workin' a heap on his copper prospect; been clawin' out a lot of ore. Had a lot of men there, diggin'. Laid 'em off for some reason. But their pay goes on just the same.

"He was tellin' me that he'd admire to find somebody that'd take 'em off his hands a while. He's got wagons there, too; plenty of them. It seems to me, that if I was figgerin' on doin' any buildin', I'd ride over an' have a talk with Jay.

"An' then," Dobble added as Burgess got into the saddle, "I don't know how I come to think of it, but Abe Jason, over in Fillets, has got an awful stock of lumber on hand lately. Seems he's been expectin' a boom somewheres. It's because of the new railroad, most likely."

Burgess urged Darkey on a few steps, but brought him to a halt when he heard Dobble speak again.

"Burgess," he said, "I reckon since you had that failin' out with Dawley you don't take no interest in Paro any more."

"Plenty of interest," said Burgess.

"Well," said Dobble, "that's good. I was afraid you'd be forgettin' Paro. You ain't had no news for a long time, though, I reckon. A man was tellin' me yesterday that Dawley's been a heap active lately in real estate. He's bought up every foot of land within two miles of Paro. Lookin' for a boom, most likely, eh?

"Dawley's runnin' back and forth between Paro an' Phoenix a lot lately, I hear. Seems someone was tellin' me he was makin' a little pasear over there tomorrow night, leavin' on the evenin' stage. Judge Quinn ain't goin', though. An' Mogridge is away; won't be back for two or three days."

After Burgess had gone, Dobble and Davis sat for a long time, looking at each other.

CHAPTER FIFTEEN

Midnight found Burgess at the Hammond ranch. Hammond met him at the door. It seemed to Burgess that Hammond was not surprised to see him, and he led Burgess inside, lighted a lamp, and for an hour they talked. When Burgess took leave, Hammond's face was beaming with satisfaction.

"I can send you fifty men, countin' the cowhands that I can spare for a time," said Hammond. "An' seven wagons, with double teams. I'll send the men over; they'll leave before daylight. You want the wagons to go right to Fillets? Lordy, you're goin' to make the fur fly!"

Burgess mounted Darkey and rode away toward Fillets. Shortly after daylight he was talking with Abe Jason.

"Lumber?" said the latter, grinning at Burgess. "Scads of lumber. *An'* brick, an' hardware! I been takin' time by the forelock, as the sayin' is. Ready to furnish all kinds of buildin' material—not classy, but substantial. For why did I stock up? Why, man, the railroad's comin' through this country, an' any man which looks ahead is goin' to be a damned millionaire! Teams an' wagons I ain't got, though. You'll have to furnish them."

After Burgess had told him what sort of building material he wanted, and had named the quantity, and inquired about the price, telling Jason he would pay for it at once, Jason looked at him meditatively and scratched his head.

"Sure. A cash deal is the sort of a deal that makes things boom," he said. "An' I ain't got no objections to takin' your money right now. But neither am I a heap afraid to trust a man which is goin' to cash in on a bonanza. Besides, 1 knowed your dad."

Burgess paid for the material, however, and Jason's eyes bulged at the size of the rolls of bills that Burgess produced.

"You must have robbed a bank, young man!" he said.

"Yes," grinned Burgess. The grin broadened when Jason gasped.

It was afternoon when Burgess got back to the cache. About seventy men, including Kuneen and his followers, were demolishing the shanties. They had found tools in one of the stores, and Hammond's men had brought more.

A number of the buildings were already down; the material from which they had been constructed had been placed in neat piles against the time when it could be used in connection with the new stuff that was to come. Other buildings were being battered to pieces; men were shouting and laughing as they worked. The cache had been turned into a human beehive.

Kuneen, hatless and coatless, was directing the work, and when he saw Burgess coming he grinned like a boy absorbed in some new game.

"Gentlemen, be ca'm!" he said. "We're raisin' hell! Before night there won't be no sign of any of these old shanties left, except the stores! Oh, how I love you, you old son-of-a-gun!"

Burgess tied Darkey with the other horses, and then with Kuneen and several other men—among them a young construction engineer who had been engaged by Hammond to erect buildings on the Hammond mining property and to superintend the erection and installing of the mining machinery on Hammond's newly discovered copper claims—spent the afternoon driving stakes.

By night a town site had been laid out, its one street running east and west, in a line that would approximately parallel the railroad that was soon to come.

The site was not a pretentious one. The town at first would not be large, nor would the new buildings be marvels of architecture or of substantialness. But town and buildings would be a monument to the indomitable resolution of a man in whom the fires of retaliation burned; they would mark the beginning of an era of grim, sturdy resistance to the evil force which had ruled Paro City and its surroundings for many days.

When twilight began to steal over the land, and the men, supping frugally upon supplies found at the cache and brought by Hammond's men, had congregated in groups, tired but filled with the fighting spirit they had caught from Burgess, several blots appeared at a distance out of the northern haze.

Kuneen was the first to catch sight of them.

"There come the wagons from Fillets!" he yelled. "There'll be plenty of work to do tomorrow, boys!"

But for Burgess there was work to do that night. For a while he watched the men, standing a little back from the light of the fires they had built. While the men laughed and talked around the wagons that had just come in from Fillets, heavily loaded down with lumber, food, tools, blankets, tarpaulins, and other necessities, he spread a blanket under a tree at the edge of the clearing, stretched out, and went to sleep.

It was almost midnight when Burgess rose and looked around him. Kuneen and two other men were sitting on their blankets near a fire. Kuneen, thought Burgess, was taking no chances against a night surprise from the exiled outlaws of the Denby band, or from the Dawley men.

Kuneen saw Burgess almost as soon as Burgess saw him, and he was walking toward Burgess by the time the latter had got the blanket on Darkey.

"Going away?" queried Kuneen.

"Riding for my health," grinned Burgess.

Kuneen stared incredulously. Then he grinned.

"The Bowen shack ain't more'n a thousand yards away, I reckon."

"Visiting my girl at midnight! I reckon she'd sure think I'd gone loco."

"I ain't sure you ain't," said Kuneen. "A man that ain't done any more sleepin' than you've done for a couple of nights might be accounted loco when he gits up in the middle of the night to go gallivantin' around the country. Goin' alone?"

"I'm wanting to do a lot of thinking," said Burgess. He had saddled Darkey by this time, and he swung into the saddle.

"I'll be back before daylight, Kuneen. So long."

He urged Darkey away from his friend and rode westward. Kuneen's gaze followed him until he vanished into the luminous mist that a rising moon spread over the plains.

"He's goin' to Paro!" muttered Kuneen lowly. "What for, I ain't got no idea. But there'll be hell to pay if anybody gits in his way, interferin' with what he's thinkin' of doin'!"

Paro City in the vicinity of the Dawley saloon and dance hall was aglitter with lights long after midnight. The City Hotel, across the street from the bank, was illuminated, as upon another night when a man had defied the law, with a single lamp that flickered on the counter near a sleepy night clerk.

There were no other signs of life on Paro's street. Westward of the saloons and dance hall only one light glimmered through a window. This was dimmed, as though it trickled between the edges of a curtain, and after a time the rider recognized the building as the courthouse. Toward the courthouse, after a short wait, he rode.

He rode to a point within perhaps a hundred feet of it, left his horse, with the reins trailing over its head, behind a thick clump of scrub oak—at which he glanced twice intently, so that he would recognize it quickly. Then he walked stealthily toward the courthouse and looked into the window through which the light shone.

Inside, sitting at a desk, in an attitude of utter dejection, was Judge Quinn.

Judge Quinn had been meditating upon the mistakes of his past. He regretted them keenly, for they had not brought him those many blessings and luxuries for which he had craved.

Tonight, and for many nights, he had been oppressed with a vivid recollection of the face of Clay Burgess when, just before he had backed out of the courthouse door on a well-remembered day, he had looked into Judge Quinn's eyes, his own expressing the disgusted contempt that honesty and straight dealing feels for dishonesty and deceit.

There had been more in Burgess' eyes—pity. For many days the judge had puzzled over that expression.

Therefore, when after a time the judge raised his head and turned at a slight sound that reached him from the direction of the door, and saw that the door had been opened and closed again, with Burgess standing just inside, a pistol in hand, his eyes glowing, his jaw queerly set, the judge was not surprised, but merely dismayed. For he had not expected Burgess to come in just that way.

But he made no sound as Burgess advanced. He was rather satisfied, in a vague, dread way, that Burgess *had* come. For now that Burgess was here the judge knew why he had not been able to sleep for many nights; why he had been in the habit of coming to the courthouse and sitting there half the night.

It was because he had expected Burgess. And this apparition was quite as dreadful as he had expected it to be. He was frozen with a terror, paralyzing and voiceless, and he watched Burgess with a gaping fascination as the latter stepped forward and halted within an arm's length of him.

"I'm back, you see," said Burgess. His smile was mirthless, giving the judge just a glimpse of his teeth. They were set.

"Back to square a long-standing account with you, Judge. It's got to be squared. I'm in something of a hurry. Can you write?" His lips curled at the judge's affirmative nod. "Write, then," ordered Burgess. "Write a statement to the effect that Mogridge killed Dal Coleman."

He stood, leaning forward a little, while the judge wrote what he had been directed to write. Then, when the judge signed it and held the paper toward him, he took the paper, folded it, and stuck it into a pocket.

"Now show me the records you keep here!" he commanded. He laughed coldly. "Paro City has been having too much law. After tonight it will have to get along without any."

The judge shivered. But he got up, walked to a safe, and drew out a number of books, which he tremblingly laid on the desk. Burgess opened book after book, tossing them aside when he noted they were not the ones he wanted. Burgess came to two, presently, that he laid beside him, placing a hand on them.

"The court and land records," he said. "I want them. I'm going to take them." He peered intently at the judge, whose ashen face was wrinkled and wreathed in lines of fear and remorse.

"I think I ought to kill you," Burgess went on. "A crooked judge is an abomination, and should be sent where he couldn't do any harm. But I've an idea that you are not as crooked as you are weak. And I'm going to let you live. Away from here. Paro City is not going to have any more of your kind of law.

"You'll go. And we'll take a chance on Dawley finding another like you. They're not plentiful, thank Heaven. You've got half an hour, Judge. I'll wait that long. Then, if you're still here, you'll stay forever."

He looked again at the judge, with a probing, searching gaze. And the judge saw reflected there again that expression which had so long eluded him, pity.

There ensued a long silence, during which the judge let his chin fall on his chest, while the tinge of shame and humiliation grew deeper on his face.

Burgess broke the silence. His voice was hoarse and strained. "You damned fool! You're not a crook at all; you're a putty ball that Dawley has been shaping for his own use!"

He seized the judge by an arm, and shook him, jerking the man toward him so that the judge staggered.

"You got a horse?" demanded Burgess. "Well, get it. Ride like hell to Dry Bottom, where you can get a train east. Get away where Dawley can't get his hands on you again. Get a new start. Be a man!" He drew some bills out of a pocket and pressed them into the judge's hand.

"There; that will help you to straighten up. Now get going. No," he added as the judge tried to speak; "you can thank me best by giving some other poor devil a square deal."

He reached over, put out the light, and dragged the judge to the door. A little later, with the two record books under an arm and the judge riding beside him, Burgess rode eastward toward the cache, deeply satisfied.

CHAPTER SIXTEEN

Burgess returned to the cache before daylight. He had ridden some miles past the cache with the judge, seeing him well on his way toward Dry Bottom, and learning from the repentant man something of Dawley's activities during the time the judge had been at Paro City.

Dawley, the judge said, owned or contolled in one way or another nearly every foot of land in the town. He had not been successful in getting control of some of the copper claims in the vicinity, and none of the property would be valuable unless the railroad came through Paro.

The Burgess estate, the judge said, was in an involved condition through Dawley's raids on it. The ranch had not been touched, so far as he knew; but other property, or the proceeds from it, had been diverted to Dawley's pockets.

Some other land belonging to the Burgess estate was distant from Paro and unencumbered in any way. This Dawley had not touched. Burgess could discover its location and status by examining the records in his possession.

But Burgess did not take time to search the records. His thoughts now were centered upon a swift, merciless campaign against Dawley and Paro City. Arriving at the cache, he secreted the records in one of the stores. Then, responding lightly to Kuneen's delighted greetings, he secured an hour's sleep.

At daylight he was up with the men, aiding in the work of construction.

Blacky Pitt returned during the day. He had lingered for a little while in Dry Bottom. Belle Carson had gone east, and he had met Judge Quinn traveling toward Dry Bottom.

"Friend of yourn now, ain't he?" grinned Pitt significantly.

The railroad was several miles west of Dry Bottom, Pitt said, and a dozen gangs of men were working hard. Some surveyors were not more than a dozen miles from the cache, and working toward it.

By noon the cache had lost all resemblance to the outlaw camp. The framework of half a dozen buildings reared upward, a half-dozen more were started, and a gang of men, under the supervision of Hammond's young engineer, were laying a pipe-line to the river, and erecting a windmill upon which the new town would depend for its water supply. One, standing almost anywhere near by, looking at the skeleton of the town, could visualize it completed.

Shortly after noon two merchants of Paro City rode up and asked to see Burgess. The latter smiled at them when he came near.

"Some different, eh?" he said, indicating the new buildings.

"Yes, some," answered one of the men. "I'm Bolton," continued the man. "I run the general store in Paro. This!"—indicating his companion "—is Bill Cartwright, who runs an eating house over there." He grinned. "We're gettin' a little tired of Paro City. We're lookin' ahead a little mebbe, too. We've been wonderin' if there's any truth in what Harvey Dobble's been sayin'."

"About what?"

"About you offerin' a buildin' an' a buildin' site free to any man now livin' in Paro which wants to move out of there an' come over here."

"Yes," said Burgess; "it's all truth. But there's a condition."

The other grinned sarcastically, and looked disappointedly at his companion.

"There's always some scheme in a deal like this. But I'm tellin' you this," he went on, his grin growing wide and admiring; "You've got the speed, young man, an' you're makin' Paro set up an' take notice. There's a volyum of gab bein' reeled off over there that'd make a Kansas twister hide in a cellar for shame.

"Somehow, folks over there has got the idea that the new railroad ain't comin' through Paro after all. An' they're wrigglin' and squirmin' around like hens on a hot griddle, wonderin' if it ain't about time to jump. They're a heap fussed an' puzzled. Something is wrong, an' the folks in Paro is about ready to stampede. If they was any truth in what old Dobble said, if you'd sure house every man that left his shack over there to come over here, they wouldn't be nobody in Paro tomorrow night except Dave Dawley an' his plug-uglies!"

"Dobble was right," said Burgess quietly. "Any man who owns a house in Paro now can have a house here, free, if he gets here within three days. First come, first served."

"You're foolin'!" gasped the man.

"Take me up," invited Burgess.

Bolton continued to stare at Burgess. And at last the light of belief glowed in his eyes.

"By God, I believe you mean it!" he said.

"Start moving," said Burgess. "There are some of the buildings going up. Would any of them suit you?"

"The second one," said Bolton, his eyes gleaming.

"It's yours—if you are in it within three days. Go and put your name on it." He looked at the other man—Cartwright. "You choosing, too?"

"The one next to Bolton's," grinned the other.

"It's yours. Move in in three days," said Burgess.

"Holy smoke!" breathed Bolton. "I've heard of such things, but this is the first time I ever run plumb into it. There's been boom towns in this country—*an'* boom towns. Towns that have sprung up overnight, an' towns that have busted overnight—everybody stampedin' out an' leavin' the buildin's to the homed toads an' rattlesnakes.

"But them other boom towns was fizzles alongisde of what this here town will be when folks finds out you mean business! Say, you ain't been chawin' no loco weed, have you? It ain't natural for a man to do a thing like this without him havin' an ace up his sleeve!"

"My ace is a half-section of land right here," Burgess told him. "The sites I'm giving away won't come anywhere near taking a quarter of it. This town is going to grow. The railroad will miss Paro by ten miles. Paro is dead, and this new town, which is to be called Burgess, will bury it. There are copper claims all around here. There won't be any spurs built to Paro. Paro is dead, Bolton, and one day I'm going over there to write its epitaph! Get busy and haul your things over here."

Late that night one of the Carey boys rode to the cache with word that Carey wanted to talk with Burgess. Burgess rode back with him, and Carey met them at the porch. Carey's face was grave and inscrutable.

"Them railroad surveyors have got to my land," he said. "I sent a bunch of the boys out to hold them off till I seen what you wanted to do about it. The surveyors have got orders for as far as Williams' cache, but they don't know what's goin' on west of that. They're waitin', though—campin' just off the line of my land. Their boss sent word to me that the general manager of the road is in Dry Bottom now, an' that it'd be a mighty good plan for me to ride over an' have a confab with him. But I wanted you with me."

At noon the next day Burgess and Carey were sitting opposite the general manager in the latter's private car, which had been shunted on a switch in Dry Bottom.

The general manager smiled a greeting to Carey, giving him a hearty handclasp. His grip of Burgess' hand was more formal. And now, as he sat opposite Burgess at the little leather-covered table, he smiled dryly as he looked him over.

"So this is the man who is fighting Dave Dawley?" he said.

"The man who is whipping him," corrected Burgess, with a straight look at the general manager.

"Well, yes," he said. "Judging from what you have already done—and are doing—you will whip him. But beware. Dawley is a resourceful fighter. But that is your affair."

He smiled.

"What we are here for is to settle the question of our right-of-way. My chief surveyor tells me that Mr. Carey won't permit him to go through the Three Bar range. We are willing to attempt to adjust any difference of opinion that may exist. What is it, Mr. Carey?"

"Burgess will do the talkin'," said Carey.

The general manager looked expectantly at Burgess.

Burgess returned his gaze steadily.

"The railroad gets a free right-of-way through the Three Bar, and through Williams' cache, if the company agrees to follow, as straight as possible, a line from Williams' cache to Las Vegas," said Burgess.

The general manager looked grave.

"And if the railroad doesn't agree?" he said.

"The road won't go through."

"Very definite and quite understandable," said the other, still grave of face. "You will fight. You seem to know something of the confused condition of affairs in the disputed land in the vicinity of the cache. I like a fighter," he added, smiling at Burgess and winking at Carey. "But I haven't any desire to lock horns with you over this question. Indeed, it isn't necessary,

Burgess. For the railroad company has no intention of going through Paro City.

"There was some talk about it a while back. And I believe certain influential persons did try to bring pressure to bear on the company to force the railroad to go through Paro. But the inducements were not great enough to offset the extra expense the road would be put to in order to bend our line to include Paro."

There it was—the word that insured the ultimate victory of Burgess over Dawley, so far as the route of the railroad was concerned. And for a long time Burgess sat silent, seeking to grasp the significance of it.

"Well," he said at last, a little hoarsely, "that seems to end the matter, doesn't it?"

He shook hands with the general manager, and with Carey trailing him, sought his horse and mounted it.

That night he rode up to the Bowen cabin, having ridden the seventy miles with no thought of fatigue and with no conscious exertion. For a strange exultation filled him. The one great problem over which he had puzzled for months had been removed with a word, and there was nothing left but a personal man-to-man fight with Dawley.

And the exultation came with the consciousness of the imminence of victory, of the certain knowledge that there was now no chance for Dawley to invoke the aid of the great company which was shoving the tentacles of civilization westward.

He could now carry the fight to Dawley, knowing that the odds against him were not too great.

He routed Ben Davis and Della out, and when they came to the door he shook Davis' hand until the old man cursed in protest; and he hugged Della so heartily that the girl looked at him in startled wonder and anxiety. Then he released her and stepped back, his eyes alight with enthusiasm.

"Jumpin' Joseph!" growled Davis resentfully. "You act like you'd discovered a gold mine!"

"I have!" responded Burgess, laughing. "And I'm going to run a railroad right in front of its door!"

CHAPTER SEVENTEEN

The new town of Burgess lay twenty miles from Paro City in a northeastward direction. No trail had led from Paro to the cache, for those who had had business at the cache had been few, and the outlaws that met and lived at the rendezvous were not followers of trails.

But within three hours from the time Burgess had talked with Bolton and Cartwright a heavily loaded wagon, drawn by four horses—which Bolton drove—was creeping over the big level, circling knobs and swinging around draws, avoiding soft stretches—breaking a trail that weaved in and out with amazing eccentricity, but with equally astounding consistency straightening each time toward Burgess.

Later Cartwright, behind another double team, with a wagon loaded as heavily as the one Bolton rode in, set out to follow the tracks made by Bolton. Still later—heading into the fading northern light—half a dozen horsemen clattered their animals in the wake of the trail-breakers. These horsemen were Paro merchants who had listened to the siren voice of golden opportunity—which seemed to come with authority from the mouth of Harvey Dobble.

A fever of unrest had seized upon Paro City. The vague rumors which had associated Paro's future with the railroad had remained vague. There were no visible signs that Paro was to profit by the coming of the railroad; there were no indications that the railroad was coming to Paro. There was, however, proof that the railroad would reach the new town of Burgess.

Annoying and provocative of disquiet was the news that trickled across the plains from the new town. The first news of a new deal at the cache had reached Paro through the medium of the women ejected by Burgess and his men. They, stopping at Paro only long enough to take the stage, had communicated the story of Denby's death and the subsequent exiling of the outlaws.

They had repeated Burgess' warning to them, "Don't stay long at Paro," and the subtle significance of the words gave the citizens of Paro much to think about. There were those who said it was "four-flush"; but there were many who strongly suspected that concealed in the words was a warning that Paro was to suffer the fate the cache had suffered.

Following quickly upon the news of the death of Denby came word of the demolishing of the old shanties of the cache and the beginning of the new building operations. This word was brought by Jay Hammond. Dobble corroborated it—with suitable additions.

It was really Dobble who sowed the seed of unrest in Paro. It was Dobble who first flatly declared that the railroad was not to come through Paro; and it had been Dobble who had quietly communicated to some favored few in Paro the news that Burgess was offering building sites and buildings gratis to men in Paro who wanted to take advantage of the future prosperity of the new town.

There was not a man in Paro who did not foresee what was to happen to Paro if the railroad did not come. Bolton was not the only man who had seen towns—many of them larger than Paro—deserted in a night; their buildings, like forlorn husks, to remain empty, desolate, rotting.

There were men who sneered when they saw Bolton and Cartwright set out into the level that stretched between Paro and the new town. They predicted, with crafty, knowing smiles, that the two men would return, after discovering that Burgess had been deceiving them.

And yet, stirring the hearts of the doubters was a fear that Paro City was "dead"—as Bolton had said, repeating Burgess' derisive word—and that the new town was to grow and flourish near its ruins.

The fear grew to a conviction which at first stunned and then reacted, afflicting the citizens of Paro with nervous indecision. And then, when still more citizens followed the example of Bolton and Cartwright, and the trail between Paro and the new town began to become well defined, and animated with wagons creeping always toward the new chance—which is ever the El Dorado of Hope in a new country—the doubters became enthusiasts and yielded to the general panic. The eastward movement grew.

On the second day it assumed the proportions of a general exodus; on the third day the exodus became a rout, with the new trail jammed with men, horses, and vehicles of all descriptions—a pushing, shoving, jostling, cursing, laughing, and shouting mass, each man afflicted by a fear of being the last to reach the haven that opportunity offered.

The new town was indescribably busy. It became a bedlam of thundering noise and clatter. It represented the energy of men imbued with the spirit to build, to grow, to expand. It was alive, teeming, ambitious. It represented the spirit of the republic—the resolution to create and to hold.

A dozen or so deputies of Mogridge and friends of Dawley remained in Paro. They roamed dazedly through the deserted buildings, picking up what articles of value remained after their owners had taken the things most needed by them.

One or two of the men tried to be jocose. But levity had no edge. Confronting them was the bare, bald fact that Paro was dead, as Burgess had predicted. And there is no humor in death.

Mogridge, returning to Paro from a little trip, did not notice at first what had happened, though it had occurred to him that the town was rather quiet. He saw several men in front of the bank building, and toward them he rode. While on his way he noted the vacant buildings, with their open doors, and the eloquent emptiness behind them. He was pale and staring when he halted his horse near the men and looked down at them.

"What in hell's happened?"

"We're holdin' down a busted camp," said one of the men. "The damned town has sloped!"

The story of the exodus, related to Mogridge by the men, left the latter nervous. Together, the men went to the courthouse and sat on the benches and chairs, looking at one another.

"Where's the judge?" demanded Mogridge, when his brain began to clear a little.

"Ain't seen him for three or four days," returned one of the men. "It's likely he got wise an' pulled his freight while the trail was empty. He couldn't have pulled out while the rest was goin'—there wasn't room."

In the courthouse Dawley found the men when he reached Paro that afternoon.

He came in, white as Mogridge had been. But, unlike Mogridge, he had divined instantly what had happened.

His pallor was the pallor of rage. He was dead white. The muscles of his mouth were twitching; those of his throat and jaws were corded and straining. His voice was hoarse and quavering when he spoke:

"When did it happen?"

"It's been happenin'. For three days. Burgess give 'em all free sites an' buildings, an' they took him up, looks like," said Mogridge.

Dawley's voice snapped:

"Where's Quinn?"

"Quinn's sloped, too."

"Gone to the cache?"

"I don't reckon he did. I missed him before the rest began to pull out. It's likely he hit the breeze some time before that."

Dawley's teeth clicked. He said nothing, but went to the safe and knelt before it, working at the combination. Presently he swung the door open and scattered the contents over the floor. He got up after a moment, his lips curving with a bitter smile.

"The records are gone," he breathed, his voice vibrating. "They're of no value to Quinn. Burgess has them. Damn your souls!" he exploded. "Why didn't you watch?"

For an instant it seemed he would leap at Mogridge, and that individual's face whitened, and his right hand opened, clawlike, and was poised just over the butt of his gun.

The other men stiffened, and they watched Dawley with sullen looks. They had no real sympathy for him, and the game was no longer worth his arrogance.

Dawley may have understood. He sneered, hesitated, and grinned coldly.

"Bah!" he said. "It wouldn't have happened if I had been here!" He went out, and the men looked at one another in silence.

In a short time Dawley returned.

"It's a sure-enough cleanout," he said, with a ghastly attempt at a smile. "But this thing has only begun. Does that damned fool think he can beat me that easily? You boys stay here and watch the bank. I'm going to Phoenix."

In the afternoon of the next day Dawley was closeted with the governor. The latter spread his hands, palms upward, when he saw Dawley.

"I'm afraid we lose, Dawley. Washington has taken the thing out of my hands—if it ever was in them. The influence of the railroad crowd, I suppose, outweighed my suggestions. I'm beginning to become convinced that we took too much for granted, in the first place."

"Then the road is going to miss Paro? It's going through the cache and straight to Las Vegas?"

"Yes."

Dawley glowered out of a window, his face dark with wrath. After a time he laughed discordantly.

"I'm pinched," he said. "Every nickel I own is tied up in land around Paro. I bought everything I could get my hands on." He turned to the governor, saying: "But I can win yet. There's only one man in my way—Burgess. He's at the cache. He's an outlaw. He killed a man named Dal Coleman in Paro. There are two witnesses—myself and Mogridge. Quinn has sneaked out of the country, or has been driven out, which is the same thing, so far as we are concerned. He took the records of his court with him. I want you to send a judge over to Paro—one that we can use—to replace Quinn. I want you to send a detail of soldiers from Fort Union. I'll get Burgess, if I have to wipe the cache off the face of the earth!"

"Crooked judges are scarce, Dawley. I don't know of another that I would dare send you. You'll have to find Quinn or go without. And I simply can't issue any orders to the post at Fort Union; that's an arm of the federal service, and they'd laugh at me. You might use Mogridge and a posse to get Burgess, but that's dangerous because the cache is out of my jurisdiction. I'm afraid you are up against it, Dawley; I'm—I'm afraid you are licked!"

Dawley got up.

"Not by a damned sight!" He glared at the governor. "I'm licked as far as you are concerned, I suppose. You always were a weak sister when it came to nerve. I'll have several things to say to you when this thing is over. Just now I'm too much in a hurry to tell you just what!"

"Dawley," soothed the governor, "you know what I'd like to do. But my hands are tied."

By this time Dawley was at the door. He sneered contemptuously at the other, slammed the door behind him, and went out, his lips in a vicious sneer.

CHAPTER EIGHTEEN

The relations of Dawley and Burgess to each other had been reversed. Through his coup in desolating Paro City, Burgess had compelled Dawley to take the offensive.

And Dawley accepted the inevitable with dogged determination. There was no thought in his mind of the surrender that the governor had hinted at.

He had never considered methods in fighting Burgess, nor any other man, and his thoughts on the trip back to Paro City were abysmal.

He had ridden his horse to Yuma; he rode it from Yuma back to Paro City, arriving there on the morning of the fourth day after leaving.

Mogridge and the other men were still there, and it required no words from Dawley to tell them that their chief had definitely determined to fight the thing out with Burgess.

Dawley's first words to Mogridge were terse and sharp:

"Send Murray and Corlett to find Denby's gang. Have them find out how many there are of them. Let them know that I've something big on hand, and that they'll come in heavy on the divvy. Tell Murray and Corlett to hustle!"

"They'll be at Dugan's Wells, most likely," Mogridge told Murray and Corlett a moment later, when he came upon the two in one of the vacant saloons. "Make it strong to them, because they're not overly in love with Dawley, anyway—an' they might hang off. Hustle! The boss is sure some disturbed!"

After Murray and Corlett left, Dawley and Mogridge sat for a time in the courthouse talking. Dawley did not refer to the project he had in mind, maintaining a silence on that subject that aroused Mogridge's wonder.

Later, Dawley and Mogridge went to Dawley's rooms above the bank, where they sat most of the day, drinking and playing cards. Twice during the play Dawley got up and looked out of the window at the deserted street, and each time he came back from the window scowling, his face flushed, impotent rage swelling his veins.

The day dragged. The sepulchral silence that lay over the town finally got on Dawley's nerves, and he got up and paced back and forth in the rooms, cursing lowly.

Dawley slept alone, Mogridge and the others bunking in the shacks they had always occupied in Paro, which had been left undisturbed by the departing citizens.

Dawley was restless. About midnight he got up and looked out into the street. Across from him loomed the dark outlines of the two-story building formerly known as the "City Hotel." The crude sign, still extending across the top of the door, was still there. But the interior was blank and dark, and Dawley found himself wishing for the companionable little nightlight that more than once he had seen shining through one of the front windows.

On the morning of the second day following their departure Murray and Corlett returned.

"They're at Dugan's Wells," Murray repeated to Dawley. "Pete Brannon is runnin' things. I felt him out. He says Burgess treated him well, an' he ain't got no kick comin' because him an' the others had to get out of the cache. Says he knowed all along that Burgess would trim you. An'—" Murray paused and looked at Dawley with embarrassment.

"Well?" prompted Dawley.

"Brannon was a heap sarcastic. He said that if you were licked so bad you wanted to join the gang, you could come over an' talk things over with him."

Dawley's face grew black with wrath, and Murray hurriedly left him.

Dawley kept to his rooms during the greater part of the day, but toward dusk he joined the men in the street.

Dawley had been brooding over what Murray had told him. He had never liked Murray, though he had known him for a dependable man. Yet it was not the first time that Murray's subtle sarcasms had irritated him. Although he knew that the members of the Denby gang had little love for him, he had expected they would be eager to cast their lot with him against the common enemy, and the discovery that the Denby men treasured no ill-feeling for Burgess filled him with a passionate rage. That rage was intensified by his dislike of Murray. The fact that Murray had repeated the sarcasm showed that Murray enjoyed it. Therefore, in his present vicious mood the thing assumed the nature of a personal insult.

Dawley was most dangerous when he seemed the most suave and gentle. Murray, knowing him long, should have been warned when, on joining Mogridge and the others in the street, Dawley stepped close to him, smiling.

"The bearer of bad news never finds favor—does he, Murray?" he said softly. "And when he takes delight in repeating a particularly bad remark he deserves—this!"

Without warning—with a rapid, driving movement that brought every muscle of his body into play, he drove a fist into Murray's face. The fist struck Murray under the chin with a force that would have shivered a plank. Murray's jaws cracked, his head snapped backward, and he sagged into a heap at Dawley's feet.

The other men stiffened, two or three of them muttering sullenly in protest. Corlett—Murray's companion on the trip to Dugan's Wells, and known to Dawley as Murray's friend, leaped up, his face working with bitter, unrestrained passion, a hand clawing at his gun.

Dawley, cool and alert, merciless, had foreseen Corlett's championship of his friend. And while Corlett, blind with rage, was pulling his gun, Dawley's weapon, flashing from his hip and held close to his side, was belching death for Corlett. Corlett's gun went off twice as he fell, the bullets splaying the sand at Dawley's feet.

Dawley wheeled slightly, facing the other men.

"Murray got fresh, and I punished him," he said. "Corlett has been itching for a gunfight for a long time. If there is anyone else who thinks I am licked, let him say so!"

Dawley's eyes were wanton with passion as they swept the faces of the other men. Divining that his outburst was a manifestation of the intense and bitter disappointment that seethed in Dawley over the realization that all his plans had miscarried and that he was facing defeat, the men were careful to make no movement that could be construed as hostile or even disapproving.

No man accepted his invitation. On the contrary, one man, who had never liked Murray or Corlett, grinned felinely, saying:

"I reckon them guys know who is boss, now!"

Another man forced a laugh. Others nodded, as though in confirmation of the first man's words.

Dawley watched, standing a little to one side, while the men took Corlett's body away. When they returned, Dawley stood, gun in hand, watching Murray, who was beginning to revive.

When Murray struggled and sat up, it was to see Dawley standing over him, menacing, mocking.

"Fell better, Murray?" he said.

Murray got up, slowly and painfully. His gun was in its holster, but he made no move toward it. The blow had cowed him completely. He shrank from Dawley, as he got up, staggering, bewildered. Dawley watched him, narrowly, grinning, until he was certain that Murray's mind was working normally again. The other men looked on, the dread in their eyes betraying their conviction that Dawley would kill Murray.

But Dawley's furious rage had spent itself, and it pleased him to be merciful to Murray.

"You're through here, Murray," he said. "You appreciated Pete Brannon's humor. Go, join him. Get out of here—quick!"

Murray looked dazedly around, seeming hardly to comprehend what had happened to him. Then he began to back away from Dawley, terror so plain in his eyes that the other men laughed in ghastly mirth.

They watched while Murray staggered to his horse and climbed into the saddle. And their eyes followed his progress as he rode down the street, eastward, veered slightly south at the street's end, and went clattering away in a cloud of dust, vanishing finally in the deep dusk that had fallen.

CHAPTER NINETEEN

Della Bowen had not been in ignorance of what had been going on at the cache. Davis and Dobble had provided her with the news of Burgess' activities.

She had not been able to participate in Burgess' fight against Dawley, further than to give him that moral support which—he told her—he appreciated more than the physical aid that could have been rendered by a thousand men. Which statement, she told him, was gross exaggeration. She still remembered the light in his eyes when he had reaffirmed the extravagance, and by that light she knew that he at least appreciated her more than a little.

Yes, Burgess had her moral support, and she was eager for him to win quickly. And yet there were doubts in her mind. Dawley she had estimated, and she felt that though things were apparently going against him, his resourcefulness would invent some scheme which would enable him to regain the advantage he had lost.

Nor had she forgotten how he had looked at her the day she had paid him the money Burgess had given her. The dread she felt of him was not all instinctive, for she had seen the evil intent in his eyes that day—the slumbering, speculative gleam that tells of a mind meditating abysmal passions.

She shuddered as she put out the light, intending to go to bed. Davis had not come in yet—sometimes he stayed out very late, looking after the few steers in the pasture, and he liked to linger over near the broken section of country where her father had discovered the copper. He told Della the place had a certain fascination for him.

His room, though, was at the farther end of the cabin, with another small room between that and hers. And a door led into Davis' room, so that many times she did not hear him come in at all.

Tonight, however, standing at the kitchen table in the darkened room, she heard him moving about outside. Curious, and somehow reluctant to go to bed, she lighted the lamp again, stepped to the door, and looked out.

The darkness blinded her momentarily. But the pale, cold gleam of the stars dissipated the darkness directly, and she saw, not many feet from the door, the shadowy outlines of half a dozen horses. All of them were riderless.

Thinking that Burgess and some of his friends had come, and that Burgess had stopped to talk with Davis before letting her know of his arrival, she stepped down from the threshold and advanced three or four steps toward the horses.

A sharp noise and a rapid movement coming from near a corner of the cabin brought her to a halt, and she wheeled swiftly, to see several figures struggling. They were men, and they were fighting! She heard several blows, making the queer sound that succeeds the impact of fist on flesh. And one of the men was cursing.

It was Davis! She heard his voice plainly. She saw him now—he was striking bitterly at the heads of several men who were massed about him. He saw her, also, and his voice reached her, shrill, high-pitched, carrying a dread warning:

"Run, Della! Git back in the shack! Git your rifle an' give 'em hell! It's Dawley an' his damn' imps!"

She heard a man curse horribly. And then Davis screamed:

"They've knifed me!"

Shocked to action by the queer, wailing note in Davis' voice, Della sprang toward the kitchen door.

She had almost reached it when the bulky figure of Dawley loomed in front of her. She made no sound, but tried to evade his clutching hands. She slipped sideways in the soft sand, and fell, hurting her ankle. She got up, though, as swiftly as she could, and did succeed in eluding Dawley's clutches once more. She had a wild hope that at last she was free of him, but she had not taken more than a step before she felt his arms go around her from the back, and she was hugged so tightly to him that she was almost stifled.

"You're quite active," mocked the man's hateful voice, coming over her shoulder. The sound maddened her, and she tried to squirm around. That failing, she kicked at him futilely.

She heard Davis groaning, but she could not see him, for several of the men were crowding around her, peering into her face.

One of the men, obeying Dawley's orders, tied her hands together. She fought the man, but without avail. But she did kick him, when he tied her ankles, and got a savage satisfaction out of that.

She shrieked once, knowing as she did so that it would avail her nothing, for there was little chance of anyone, excepting Dawley and his men, hearing her.

Laughing lowly, Dawley left her in charge of two of the men and entered the cabin. A little later she saw him sitting at the table near the lamp. He seemed to be writing.

Shortly afterward he came out again, after extinguishing the lamp. He loomed big and formidable in the doorway for an instant, and then he stepped forward and spoke sharply to one of the men:

"Are you sure of him?"

Evidently he meant Davis.

The man laughed shortly, brutally:

"I reckon he won't do no tattlin'."

Della sagged limply in the arms of the two men. They had killed Davis! The horror of that knowledge sent her senses skittering into chaos. But a swift reaction, in which rage was the dominant emotion, stiffened her failing muscles, and she stood erect and screamed at Dawley:

"You beast! Oh, you beast!"

Dawley laughed, walked to her, brushing the men aside, and, seizing her in his arms, kissed her fiercely, half a dozen times, full on the lips. Then, swiftly, making no more effort than if she were a child, he lifted her, carried her to his horse, mounted, with her still in his arms, and urged his horse forward, followed by the others.

Della must have fainted. She was sure of that when some time later she saw the deserted buildings of Paro City looming just ahead of her through the starlit gloom of the night. If anything more were needed to convince her, it was Dawley's mocking voice, coming again over his shoulder as they rode:

"Awake now? Well, you did go under, right! I thought, from the way you looked at me one day when I was over to visit you, that you had more spirit. Or are you afraid of me?"

She did not answer.

"Don't be," he mocked. "I don't intend to hurt you. At least, not until after I have a little scene with Burgess."

"Burgess will kill you for this!" she breathed savagely.

"No doubt you *wish* he would. But we don't always get everything we wish for."

She set her lips, determined to talk no more to Dawley. She struggled, though, to escape the tightness of his arms, but he merely squeezed her the more, and at last she gave up and endured the caressing pressure, assuring herself that on the morrow, when Burgess found her—for he had told her he would be coming tomorrow—Dawley would pay in proportion to his actions.

Reaching Paro, the men scattered; Della saw them going singly into the deserted building, first taking their rifles from the holsters on their saddles. One of the men led the horses away. All but Dawley's. The man led that animal, fully saddled and bridled, to the hitching-rail in front of the bank building.

Della made mental note of this odd performance, while she stood where Dawley had set her down, leaning against the hitching-rail.

Dawley stopped to talk for a moment to the one man among them—besides Dawley—that Della knew—Mogridge. The men spoke in whispers, and the girl could not hear what they said. But after Dawley finished he came toward Della, grinning with satisfaction.

"Well," he said, "we'll go."

He kissed her again, holding her cheeks in his hands and peering deep into her eyes, his own glowing with a passion that made the girl reel from terror.

Laughing vibrantly, he lifted her again, carried her to the door that led to the upper story of the bank building, and after climbing the stairs he opened the door of the front room, entered, and set her down.

"Well," he said. Then: "We've got this far."

He locked the door and put the key into his pocket. He found a match, lit the lamp, and in its glare stood, leaning a little forward, looking at her appraisingly.

"You're *worth* a lot of trouble, Della," he said. "No wonder Burgess took a shine to you so quickly! But I forget my manners." He walked to her, lifted her, and placed her in his favorite chair.

Della leaned back in it and closed her eyes—chiefly to keep from looking at Dawley—to shut out the sight of his smilling, triumphant eyes.

Later—she did not know how long she had sat there—she opened her eyes again, to see Dawley sitting in another chair near her, watching her.

"Look here," he said soberly, when he noted that her eyes were open. "I appreciate that this experience is hard on you. And I'll admit that I like you—very much. More than I ever liked any woman. I've got all I can do to keep from manifesting my liking for you, too—I can tell you that!

"But you are perfectly safe, in spite of that. For I want you *right* when I take you. And I won't take you until several things are settled." He narrowed his eyes at her. "I don't think there is any danger of Burgess finding you here for a few days—in spite of your threats."

Her eyes blazed with dire prophecy as she met his glance. "Burgess is coming to my cabin tomorrow morning—early. He'll find me, and he'll kill you, Dawley!"

Dawley's eyes gleamed wickedly. But he spoke smoothly:

"You shouldn't have told me that, Della. For if you hadn't, Burgess might have surprised me. I didn't know when he would be along. But I knew he *would* be coming to see you. That's why I left your little love note, lying on the table in the kitchen—your kitchen."

"My note?" She looked at him in astonishment, realizing there was something subtle and designing in his manner. "I left no note for him."

"Well," laughed Dawley, "we'll say it is my note. But it was written in your hand. I found some old letters in the cabin, and I duplicated your style as nearly as I could. Even to the signature.

And I flatter myself that I did a good job. I don't think he will detect the forgery."

"You wrote—what?" she asked, her curiosity overcoming her. Dawley smiled. "I remember it perfectly. It runs this way:

"BURGESS—

"Dawley surprised and overpowered me. He is going to take me to Paro City. He will be there alone, for I overheard him tell Mogridge and some of his men to join the remnant of the Denby gang. I haven't time to write more, for Dawley is coming. Please come for me—quickly.

DELLA"

"You lied!" charged the girl wrathfully. "For you have a dozen men here with you!"

"Yes," Dawley laughed, "a dozen. And myself—don't forget me."

Something in his manner—something vicious and cruel and sneering—made the girl look quickly at him. She caught her breath sharply.

"Oh!" she cried. "It is a scheme, a plot! You are going to lure him here—to kill him!"

"Accurate, but a little belated, Della," he mocked. "You should have divined that when I read the note I left for Burgess." His eyes grew dark with passion; he spoke huskily:

"Yes, it's a frame-up. When Burgess comes, he dies! My men are all here—secreted in the empty buildings. Some are on this side of the street, some are on the other side. They are to keep themselves hidden. But they are to be on the lookout for Burgess. They have rifles, and they will shoot Burgess on sight!

"Clever, isn't it?" he went on, while she sat rigid, looking at him, her eyes dilated and quickening with horror. "I left my horse standing in front of the bank building—so that when Burgess comes he will know where to look for me. The other horses are in a stable, down the street a ways. The appearance of the town will bear out my statement, in the note, that I am here alone—with you. Burgess will be eager, careless. He will get off his horse in front of the bank. And when he does a dozen riflemen will riddle him!"

The girl's face was pallid and drawn. Dawley had provided a vivid picture for her imagination, and she could see how readily Burgess would follow Dawley's line of reasoning. Her realization of her helplessness was acute. But words would not come—there *were* no words that could have expressed the dismay and horror she felt for the satanic cleverness of the plan that had been devised for the killing of Burgess. Nor were words adequate to express the rioting, mingled passions of hate, disgust, and the stark, naked dread she felt for the man who sat watching her with implacable, smiling eyes. He was enjoying her mental distress. With black triumph in his heart he was anticipating the success of his plan. Oh, it *would* succeed, she knew! For Burgess would come! And even now in her imagination she could hear the venomous crashing of the rifles that would send him to his death.

CHAPTER TWENTY

Though the distance from the new town to the Bowen cabin was only five miles, Burgess had not ridden it for several days—since the day before the exodus from Paro City had begun.

His time had been fully occupied. And besides, he had told Della that he would not come for a week. For he had anticipated the confusion and turmoil that would follow the incoming avalanche of men, vehicles, horses, stores, and the miscellaneous baggage that always accompanies a removal of any sort.

Confusion *had* reigned. In the first place, there had not been nearly enough new buildings to go round. Claimants of building sites had dumped their goods on the land, covered them with what protection they could provide—tarpaulins, canvas, blankets. Some mounds of goods had no covering.

Some tent-houses had been erected; other persons camped in the open. Still others camped not at all, but devoted their nights to the building of their dwellings and stores.

The atmosphere of the new town was feverish with preparation. But within the past two or three days order and system were slowly gaining the ascendancy, and the town of Burgess began to make a creditable appearance. Then, with the mammoth task well in hand, Burgess began to think of going to the Bowen cabin.

At dusk on the night Dawley had visited the Bowen cabin and carried Della away, Burgess was sitting on the porch of Denby's house, looking toward the new buildings of the town he was sponsor for. It represented effort of the most intense kind; it was a monument to danger surmounted and to a victory achieved. Yet, without Della Bowen to share the fruits of it with him, it would have been without value in his eyes. He knew, now, that had he not met Della Bowen he would not have made any effort to build the town or to attempt to force Dawley's ruin by scheming. He would merely have waited until he had recovered his strength. Then he would have ridden to Paro City, killed Dawley and Mogridge—and any others that might have attempted to obstruct his vengeance. Following that—if he came out of the mêlée with his life—he would have headed south, to be swallowed up in that vast country in which he had spent so many years of his life. Della Bowen had provided him with the incentive to fight Dawley in the manner he *had* fought him.

He kept thinking of her as he watched the lights and fires of the new town. He kept seeing her face in the dancing shadows that arose around the lights. Tomorrow he had promised to visit her. But—

He got up, grinning with an embarrassment which he knew came with surrender to the yearning that he had been combating all day and evening.

"What's a few hours—when a man wants to see his girl—and can't wait?" he asked of the surrounding silence.

Yet he did not answer it at once. Now that he had surrendered, he found himself wondering what Della would think, to see him coming in the night, many hours before the appointed time. His coming beforehand would be tacit evidence of his longing for her—and he didn't want to appear too eager.

He stepped down from the porch and sought the street of the town, walking among the mounds of goods and the groups of people, straining his ingenuity in an endeavor to devise some excuse for his appearance at the Bowen cabin.

Everywhere he was greeted with smiles and respectful attention. For by this time every potential resident of the new town
knew of his fight and sympathized with him.

He saw Kuneen and his friends, and stopped for a few words
with them. But it was after ten o'clock before he succeeded in
inventing a reason for his intended visit to the Bowen cabin. But
when he did hit upon an excuse he acted quickly.

He saddled Darkey, grinning as he did so. Then he rode the
horse stealthily through the timber, so that he could not be seen
from the town; forded the river, where it doubled; ascended the
opposite slope, and rode swiftly over the big level toward the
Bowen cabin.

It was eleven o'clock when he rode up to the door of the
cabin. He knew something of Davis' habits—having watched
the man during his seven weeks' illness—and suspected that he
would find Davis prowling around in the vicinity. He smiled at
the door—which was wide open, showing the black interior of
the kitchen—and urged Darkey on. He circled the pasture, and
rode to the section of broken country where the copper had been
found.

A trifle puzzled, wondering if she *had* gone to bed and had
left the kitchen door wide open, he returned to the cabin and sat
on Darkey in front of the door. And now, for the twentieth time,
a conviction of the absurdness of this visit assailed him.

His excuse for the visit seemed suddenly ridiculous and puer-
ile, and he was debating the propriety of returning to the cache
without making his presence known when he heard a groan.

He stiffened, an odd chill assailing him, and peered intently
toward the point from which the groan seemed to come. He saw
the figure of a man, huddled against the wall of the cabin at one
of the corners, and he slipped off Darkey, drew one of his pistols,
and strode toward it.

He recognized Davis instantly. Stooping, he went to one knee and got the man's head up, shaking him gently to arouse him—for his first impression was that Davis had been taken sick, had tried to get to his room—which was reached through a door just around the corner—and had failed, falling where he had found him.

But as his hand pressed the old man's back he felt a curious moisture. He withdrew the hand, held it up to the starlight, saw blood upon it, and felt around the spot where the moisture was heaviest.

His investigation was rapid, but thorough. Its result brought a queer stiffening to his lips.

"Knifed!" he breathed huskily.

He lifted Davis and carried him into the kitchen, laying him on the floor near the table and searching his own pockets for a match. Twice he called to Della, but there came no answer, and he lit the lamp, stripped Davis' clothing from him so that he could get at the wound, bathed the wound with water secured from the pail that stood on a bench just inside the door, and then, standing erect, he looked down at Davis and shook his head.

Turning again, to call for Della, he saw some writing material on the table—almost at his hand. One sheet of paper was slightly apart from the others, and he saw his name on it. As he snatched it up and read it the blood went out of his face, and he stiffened with a cold rigidity that told of shock, terrific and stunning.

But it was over quickly. With a bound, his eyes blazing, a glint in them like an intense flame concentrated to a pinpoint, he reached a door leading from the kitchen to another room—which he knew was Della's. Many nights during his sickness he had seen her standing before it as she said goodnight to him.

He swept it open, sending it crashing back against the wall with one vicious sweep of the arm. He peered within. The room was empty; the bed had not been slept in. He ran to Davis' room. That, too, was empty.

Grimly he returned to Davis and looked down at the man's face.

"You've got a chance, but you'll have to wait," he said to the unconscious man.

He was out of the house with one bound; in another he was on Darkey's back, and before he had traveled a dozen yards the great, rangy, spirited beast was in a dead run, his thundering hoofs spurning the sand of the big level that stretched, dimly luminous in the star haze, from the cabin to Paro City.

Burgess knew the trail, and he gave Darkey the benefit of his knowledge—keeping him to the hard, well-packed sand, guiding him away from the broken stretches, skirting the draws—where he might have lost precious seconds—sending him, flashing like a black phantom running before a whirlwind, into the black distance that yawned ahead of him.

In that heavy, distressing blackness of the night just preceding the first faint signs of dawn, Burgess caught sight of the buildings of Paro City. They loomed, somberly and desolately, in his vision as he urged Darkey to additional effort, for there is something in the look of a deserted town that oppresses the mind with a consciousness of dread finality—the emotion that afflicts one when looking at a body from which the soul has departed.

Paro's soul had gone, and the husk which had been its body remained. But a sinister, evil demon had crept into the husk.

For the first time in his life Burgess was on fire with the lust to slay. There had been a cold deliberateness in the killing of Denby and the Gopher, in the shooting of Tulerosa. And self-defense had been the motive that had prompted him to slay Dal Coleman. Yet he had done all that shooting without passion.

Now, he was vibrating with passion. The grim humor which had characterized him all his days had been whelmed by the blood lust that held him in its mighty clutch. Yet there was a coldness about him, a repressed eagerness, which indicated that his was not a furious, headlong rage, but a passion which permitted him to see and think clearly—which would be all the more deadly because it would last until he achieved his aim.

When he reached the edge of town he did not do what Dawley had expected him to do—ride down the street from the easterly end. He divined where he should find Dawley. And when he struck town he sent Darkey tearing through the back yards, leaping over mounds of refuse and heaps of tin cans that flew, clattering and rattling, away from Darkey's racing hoofs. He reached the rear of the bank building, threw himself out of the saddle, and, running down the passageway between the bank building and another on its eastward side, he made for the door in front that led upward to Dawley's rooms.

CHAPTER TWENTY-ONE

Dawley, not expecting Burgess until well toward noon of the next day—probably he would defer his visit to the Bowen cabin until afternoon—had seated himself in another big chair, not far from Della. For two hours he had tried to talk with the girl, but she had returned monosyllabic replies when she spoke at all, and Dawley had soon tired of his efforts. Then, leaving her to sit alone in the room, he went into one of the other rooms and drank several times from a decanter on a sideboard.

He drank heavily, and it affected him, for when he finally returned to the room in which Della sat his face was slightly flushed, and there was a glint of recklessness in his eyes. Twice, standing near her after returning from the other room, he looked at her with a smile full of the darkest significance, but each time he controlled himself. At last, sinking into the big chair, he settled back, watching Della.

Dawley was not accustomed to the use of intoxicants. The stress of the past few days, the spectre of defeat confronting him, had driven him to indulge in the liquor. It made him drowsy as he sat there, and two or three times he dozed off, catching himself each time and sitting, between dozes, looking at Della. Had he been fully awake within the past few minutes he could have heard the rapid drumming of hoofs on the big level near the town; he could not have failed to hear the clashing clatter of the empty tin cans that were knocked helter-skelter by Darkey's flying legs.

Della heard them. She had heard them from afar. At first only a faint sound, which advanced and receded, and advanced again. But she heard them, and their significance was unmistakable. And yet she had no hope that it was Burgess who was coming. One of Dawley's men, she supposed, having been left behind, was coming to join the others.

She listened to them, however, straining her ears to catch every slight sound, and as they came closer and grew more sharply definite and clear, she sat erect in her chair, the color going and coming in her cheeks, her eyes wide with a wild hope.

It was not until she heard the tin cans clattering that she knew someone was in a desperate hurry, and when she heard the sound of someone running down the passageway between the two buildings, a sudden presentiment that it *was* Burgess assailed her. And with a glance at the dozing Dawley she stood up, hopped lightly but quickly to one of the front windows—which was open—leaned far out, saw the man standing at the door below her, saw that it *was* Burgess, and screamed a warning to him:

"Look out, Burgess! There are men in some of the buildings—with rifles! Go away! Get help!"

She would have said more, but Dawley was upon her. One of his hands was clamped brutally over her mouth; she was seized with the other, drawn back from the window with a ferociousness that staggered her; then she was lifted and thrown with a force that sent her far back into the room, sprawling upon the floor.

In that position she heard a rifle crash—she knew it by the lingering, whiplike snap it made. Then came another shot—also from a rifle, and then several more, in a continuous stream. She struggled and sat up, murmuring a prayer that none of the bullets would hit Burgess.

She saw Dawley, standing at a little distance back from the front windows, his lips in a horrible pout, watching, listening for any sound that would tell him that his riflemen had been successful.

No sounds came. After the first succession of reports there came a heavy silence. It was broken presently by a single shot—then two more—from the opposite side of the street. By that token Dawley knew none of the bullets had found Burgess; and he cursed profanely and bitterly.

There came another silence, lasting long. Then followed the crashing tinkle of breaking glass, a heavy thump and a clatter as of someone falling and scrambling to his feet. Then came a thudding jar, a splitting, rending, thunderous crash. And then both the girl and Dawley heard rapid footsteps on the stairs!

Dawley's face had gone dead white. He moved, pantherlike, toward the door at the stair landing, drawing his pistol as he went. His teeth were set tightly, his chin in the rigid thrust of malignant resolution.

Apparently he had forgotten Della. But the girl was in a frenzy of concern for Burgess. She knew it was he whose step she had heard on the stairs; and she knew, in the tense silence that followed his arrival at the top, that he was waiting on the other side of the door to get his breath before he attempted to batter it down.

She got to her feet, noting the deadly menace in Dawley's manner. She saw his gun move slightly forward at his hip, observed the tensing of the muscles that denoted the imminence of action. Hopping, almost falling in her eagerness, she lunged against him just as he pulled the trigger of the weapon. She knew that the bullet had not gone through the door—as Dawley had intended it should—for she heard Dawley's curse as he wheeled and struck at her viciously. But he missed.

The door crashed as Dawley's gun went off, seeming to burst from its hinges. Della fell, Dawley upsetting her as he wheeled to strike her. The force with which Dawley struck threw him off his balance. Trying to recover, he tripped over the legs of the falling girl and went down sideways, on a shoulder. Della, falling, saw the door topple toward her; saw Burgess lunge through the wreck of it, blood on his face, his eyes blazing with the fury of the lust that had seized him.

Murray, still dazed and hardly comprehending what had happened to him, rode out of Paro City. Automatically—following Dawley's advice in the absence of any definite determination on his own part—he rode toward Dugan's Wells—where he would find Pete Brannon and the remnant of the Denby band.

But Murray had not ridden many miles before he began to remember. And following remembrance came a natural and bitter resentment against Dawley.

Halfway to the cache—and a little south of it, on a direct line to Dugan's Wells—he halted in a little timber grove. There the course of action was decided. By ten o'clock he was within sight of the new town of Burgess.

It was about ten-thirty when he rode in and found Kuneen.

He knew what Dawley had done to Kuneen—for he had been with Mogridge and the others when Kuneen had fought his losing fight. Also, he knew many of Kuneen's friends, and was familiar with the history of Dawley's treatment of them.

When—after telling Kuneen what he wanted to tell him—that Dawley was in Paro City with not more than a dozen men—he saw Kuneen's face whiten and his eyes leap, blazing with a deep fire, he felt that part of his debt to Dawley had been paid. And when, later, after being told by Kuneen that he might stay at the new town if he behaved himself, he saw a score of grim-faced men mounting horses—each man heavily armed—he grinned with savage satisfaction.

Still later, when the score of horsemen rode out of town toward Paro City, Kuneen at their head, he almost yielded to an impulse to follow them. But he did not follow. He curled up in his blanket near one of the fires and went to sleep, confident that he had set forces to work that would revenge him for what he had suffered at Dawley's hands.

Kuneen had organized his men with stealth. He had not seen Burgess leave the cache, and he knew that if Burgess divined what he was about to do there would be a decided objection. So he warned the men to move quietly and carefully, lest they apprise Burgess of the nature of their errand. Thus they got out of the cache with little or no disturbance and rode slowly toward Paro.

Once out of sight of the cache, however, they moved more rapidly, and with the urge of revenge in their hearts growing more compelling as they drew nearer to Paro City, their pace grew still more rapid until, coming within sight of the town, their horses were in a dead run.

And then, still nearer to Paro, the reports of firearms reached their ears. They halted long enough to make certain. And then, hearing other reports, and seeing the flame spurts streaking the darkness from the street ahead of them, they rode forward cautiously, curious and alert.

Burgess had heard Della's voice. And he had dodged back into the passageway just in time to escape the bullet which sang viciously near his head. He heard the bullet thud into the frame wall of the building next to the bank; he heard others striking the brick wall of the bank building.

But in the flashing glance he had taken of the street in front of the building he had seen Dawley's horse. And he had noted the feeble glimmer of light issuing from the window out of which Della had leaned.

The crashing of the rifles around him warned him that Dawley had set a trap for him, and he grinned with cold contempt as he retreated down the passageway, and with the butt of one of his pistols smashed a glass in one of the windows of the directors' room. He cut one of his hands getting through the opening, and fell headlong in the debris inside. The door at the bottom of the stairs had given him some trouble, but he had shivered it on the second attempt, going through it, shoulder first, and crashing against the wall on the opposite side. His forehead had struck some obstruction on the wall when he had catapulted across the lower landing, and the blood in his eyes had blinded him. He had swept it away with the hand that had been cut by the glass. But the blood from the hand, added to that already trickling down his face, created a startling effect, so that when Della saw him she was sure some of the bullets had struck him.

Burgess had drawn one of his guns. But he could not use it on Dawley. While Burgess was still in the wreck of the door, Dawley, realizing his own disadvantage, seized Della—who was lying partly across him—and swung her around so that she formed a shield for him. Then, as Burgess leaped toward him out of the wreck of the door, he shot—four times in rapid succession.

Three of the bullets went wild, because Della, sensing his purpose, twisted in his grasp and lunged against his pistol arm. Before he could pull the trigger again Burgess had kicked it out of his hand.

The rage that filled Burgess' heart was almost the cause of his undoing. He had put too much force into the kick. He slipped, and went to one knee, falling awkwardly. In throwing out his right hand to catch himself the hand struck the edge of a chair, knocking the gun out of his clutch and causing an agonizing pain to run up his arm.

He had fallen into the battered remains of the door, and as he struggled to rise, the debris caught in his clothing and hampered his movements.

Dawley, quick to take advantage of his predicament, threw Della from him. She landed, head first, against the leg of a table and lay still, stunned, while Dawley scrambled to his feet and threw himself at Burgess.

He landed, shoulder first, on Burgess, and the weight of his body again upset Burgess. He fell, flat on his back in the debris, with Dawley on top of him.

One of Dawley's bullets had struck Burgess. A fiery seam ran along his right side, under his arm. The arm had lost some of its strength, but Burgess did not spare it. He could not, for Dawley, as soon as he landed on Burgess, began to claw for the gun that still reposed in the holster on Burgess' left side.

Burgess blocked that intention with his left hand, while with his right he braced his body. Slipping his knees up to Dawley's waist, disregarding the hand that was at his throat, he lifted Dawley, using his knees as a lever, and threw the man over his head. Dawley landed on all fours, just beyond Burgess. He was up in a flash, catlike, snarling, his face hideous with passion.

It was his turn, this time, for Burgess was tardy in getting to his feet. The effort to throw Dawley over his head had cost him something in strength, and when Dawley reached his feet Burgess was on his stomach, reaching for his gun. He drew it. But again his position was awkward, and before he could twist around to get a shot at his antagonist, Dawley kicked savagely, and the gun flew from Burgess' hand and clattered to the floor out of reach.

Dawley threw himself at it. But as he went past, Burgess tripped him, and Dawley went down, the force of the fall bringing a grunt out of him.

But he was up again, and diving toward his own weapon, which had landed near the table close to where Della lay.

Seeing Dawley's intention, and realizing that he was too far from his own gun to get it before Dawley could bring his own into use, Burgess leaped for Dawley as the latter stooped. Dawley sensed the movement, and his own were lightning fast. He got the gun, and Burgess was within three feet of him when Dawley pulled the trigger. Burgess staggered as the bullet struck him, but came on, Dawley snapping the hammer of his weapon on empty shells.

Dawley's killing of Corlett had worked Dawley's ruin. With two bullets in him Burgess could not have carried another. Dawley had forgotten to reload the weapon, and the one bullet that he had fired at Corlett would have halted Burgess. But Corlett had got that one. And Dawley's last bullet did not halt Burgess, did not seem to affect him in any way.

Dawley tried to club the gun as Burgess closed with him. The hand holding it was seized and wrenched with resistless fury, and the gun thudded to the floor.

Burgess got a grip on Dawley's throat. Dawley broke it and, backing away, swung a fist heavily to Burgess' face, staggering him. Burgess came on, reeling a little, and when Dawley struck again he blocked the blow with an elbow. Dawley cursed, and his face whitened. It was the first word that had been spoken, and it brought a bitter grin to Burgess' face. For it meant that Dawley had hurt his hand, and when Burgess sent a fist smashing into Dawley's face, Dawley made no attempt to use the hand, except to try and fend off the blow.

Dawley clinched, resorting to his strength and physical condition. He had failed to correctly judge the other's implacable fury, however, and though he fought desperately, exerting to the utmost those rippling muscles that he had always admired, he could not keep Burgess' hands from slipping upward to his throat. They reached there finally, and Dawley cursed again as he felt the terrible pressure of the iron fingers. He beat the other's face desperately with his good hand, driving in blows that would have killed a normal man. But Burgess was no longer normal. Feeling had left him. He felt no sensation except a terrible, over-powering passion to kill this man who, from the very first, had tried to ruin him with his evil schemes. And he worried Dawley here and there, keeping the grip he had gained, oblivious to Dawley's sledge-hammer blows, taking no account of the retching pain that filled him, concentrating the strength of his mind and body in the effort to kill.

Down in the street streaks of flame were still splitting the darkness. Kuneen, stealing around to the rear of the bank building, had seen Burgess' horse. He ordered his men to scatter, and presently the flame streaks from the buildings grew fewer.

Kuneen's men, with the memory of many wrongs to urge them, were not to be denied. Murray had told them there were a dozen Dawley men in Paro. And Kuneen's men, surmising that Burgess and Dawley were in the rooms above the bank building, were eager to get at the man who had caused them to be outlawed. During the pauses in the firing they could hear the noise of the battle that was raging in Dawley's rooms. And fearful that Dawley would win, they took long chances. Boldly, with a cold courage that would not be balked, they entered buildings from which shots had come, hunting the shooters down, dragging their victims out.

When more than half Dawley's men had been accounted for, and only one of Kuneen's men had been struck—and that only slightly—Kuneen took a rock and shattered the door in the front of the bank building, leading to Dawley's rooms. Bounding up the stairs, gun in hand, he reached the upper door. Framed in the doorway he saw Della sitting up near a table, looking about her in bewilderment.

Beyond the table, staggering amid the wreck and ruin of the room, were Dawley and Burgess. Dawley's face was blue-black, his head was rolling oddly from side to side. And while Kuneen watched, in the grip of a dread fascination, Dawley's body sagged, then dropped quickly. Burgess stood, for a breathless instant, looking down at the form of his beaten adversary. Then, drawing a deep breath, he turned his head, slowly and painfully, and saw Kuneen.

His lips parted in a slow, wan grin.

"It's Kuneen," he said, in a smothered voice. He tottered toward the table and laid a hand on it, swaying back and forth as Kuneen, seeing his condition, stepped quickly toward him.

"Kuneen," he said, the grin still on his lips. "Della Bowen is here. And—and—I reckon—that's all."

His eyes closed, and he lurched over on the table. Before Kuneen could reach him he had slipped to the floor, where he lay, limp and lax.

CHAPTER TWENTY-TWO

A week later, Burgess City—as the town finally became known—was still in the confused condition it had been in when Burgess had left it that night to visit Della Bowen. In a week not a nail had been driven, not a board had been lifted, nor had any of the goods that littered the townsite been moved. Burgess City, so far as progress was concerned—visible progress—was exactly where it had been the week before.

For in the house formerly occupied by Flash Denby, the outlaw, lay the founder of Burgess City, making a courageous and determined fight for the life that Dawley had tried to rob him of. Moreover, he was winning. But, until the victory was assured, Burgess City would wait.

Kuneen and his men—and Della Bowen—had brought Burgess to his own town on a blanket spread between four horses. A man had preceded Kuneen and his men to Burgess City. There the man had secured a fresh horse and had ridden to the Three Bar. From the Three Bar one of Carey's sons had ridden to Dry Bottom with certain written words—from Carey—to the general manager of the new railroad—who was still in Dry Bottom. An engineer and a private car, whizzing eastward and whizzing back again at like speed, had brought a great doctor from a nearby town. That doctor, except for the few minutes he had been forced to sleep from sheer weariness, had watched at Burgess' bedside for a week.

And another person, more interested than the doctor, had watched also. There had been times when the furrows of anxiety had been deep in her face, and she had bothered the doctor with continuous questions. She bothered Ben Davis too, for Davis was in the room next to Burgess, sitting up, and very capricious.

But today the furrows could not be seen. One could see only the smile on her face. For the doctor had told her Burgess was to get well. More, the doctor had told her she might talk to Burgess as much as she pleased—that tomorrow he was going east, anyway; and that Burgess would get well in spite of her talk.

Burgess had visitors today. He was propped up in bed on several white pillows. He was pale, and all the tan was gone, and he looked a trifle drawn and weak. But there was nothing weak about the grin that he flashed at Harvey Dobble, who sat on one side of him; at Della, who was seated at the foot of the bed, watching him; and at Carey, big, bluff, who was speaking:

"Well, I ain't sayin' that you didn't make a good fight, for you did. But what I'm gettin' at is that mebbe you wouldn't have made as good a fight if things hadn't been sorta framed up for you. Lots of guys in this world do things that they get too much credit for; an' lots of fellows do a heap that they don't get any credit for. Take you. Me an' Dobble an' Ben Davis was trustees for your property. Only you didn't know it. We've took the necessary steps to drag Dawley's affairs into court an' have them straightened out. An' we've got a judge which will *be* a judge. Only, he's goin' to sit in Burgess City—which our legislature, last week, took over into this territory. Well, what I was goin' to say is that everything will be cleared up as regards your property. We know where the records are—you done a lot of yappin' about them while you was out of your head. They show regular, accordin' to the lawyer man which I brung here—an' which is goin' to stay here till everything is straightened up.

"But you was sorta independent like—an' wouldn't ask no questions about anything. Which me an' Dobble an' Davis thought we'd let you have your own way—an' mebbe you'd clean up the cache. They wasn't nothin' lost in waitin' to see what kind of a guy you was."

"He was kinda slow, I reckon," remarked Dobble.

"Yes," said Carey; "slow, I reckon he was. He let me sell him land he already owned—the half-section that the cache—that Burgess City is standin' on." He grinned at the expression in Burgess' eyes. "Yep," he added; "your dad owned it, an' willed it to you. Why didn't you look at the records when you had 'em? But," he went on, grinning widely, "I reckon I hadn't ought to have let you worry like you did about the railroad comin' through to Paro. I reckon my sister would have clawed the general manager's wool out if he'd have let that road run through Paro City—an' me not wantin' it to."

"Your sister?" said Burgess; "why, what has your sister—"

Carey guffawed. "She's been cookin' his grub for him for twenty-five years. An' he's lettin' on that he's a dutiful husband!"

"You knew all the time, then, that the road would miss Paro?" said Burgess.

"I reckon."

"Is there anything else you know—that you haven't told?" grinned Burgess.

"Why, yes." Carey looked at Della, and deliberately winked. "Now that you're in your right mind again there's somebody here that's like to do a heap of talkin' to you. We'll all go out, an' the one that stays will be the one that wants to do the gassin'."

He got up, grinning, and went out. Dobble followed him. Carey stole a glance backward when he reached the door.

A huge silence engulfed the two. It was broken by Della.

"Oh," she said softly; "it's so good to have you again!"

"I reckon you've got nothing on me, there," he smiled.

"Do you know," she asked presently, after they had been silent for a time, "what they did?"

"I haven't been doing much watching and listening," he reminded her gently.

"They—the men in Burgess City—were so enraged after—when we brought you home—and Davis—that a number of them rode over to Paro City and destroyed it!"

"How?"

"Burned it. There is nothing left standing, except the bare walls of the bank building. Everything else is entirely destroyed. I—I haven't been over there, but they say that it looks terribly desolate and lonely, and that the sand of the desert is already beginning to drift over the ruins." She shuddered. "I hate to think of it."

"Don't, then," he said. "It's a heap better to think of the future, anyway. You can think of the new town we are building here, and of the new home I'm going to build for——"

"Me," she whispered, smiling.

THE END